Star

Man's

Son

C. C. Archambeault

Star Man's Son

Printed in the United States of America by CreateSpace Publishing
Platform.

First Paperback Edition: March 2015

Juvenile Fiction / Science Fiction

Book 1 of the *Star Man's Son* series.

ISBN – 13: 978-1507683552

ISBN – 10: 1507683553

Cover design by Fiona Jayde Media.

050721

To my daughter Michelle
Thank you for your support in so many ways.

Contents

(Chapters continue on next page.)

Contents continued...

Chapter 1

Caught!

It was a warm night, but the sweat on him wasn't from the heat. He crouched low in the darkness. He did not dare show fear, even though he was terrified. The older boys convinced him that he was the only one who could carry out this dangerous mission, since he was the smallest and very quick—that's why they called him "Little Monkey." He had stolen from the Star Men before, but not from inside the Star Men's place! This would be far more dangerous. He clenched his jaw. He knew he could do this. He must do this. He had to show the others that he was equal to them.

He cautiously crept through the shadows all the way up to the steps. He raised his head for a quick peek. He saw no one, so with a deep breath, he dared to go through the open door. Inside, he crouched down as his eyes quickly surveyed the kitchen.

Then the smells overcame him. Oh! Such wonderful smells! Food! The aroma of fresh food made his empty stomach hurt all the more. The lights were on inside, but not very bright, and they cast shadows enough for him to quietly creep and then dash from one to another.

Ahead, there was a table. He couldn't help but stare. What a table! There was all manner of food upon it. He had never seen so much ready-to-eat food before in his life! Further away, several Star Men sat around another table, but they seemed to be intent on their dinner.

His heart beat fearfully as he watched them. Those Star Men! They were so big! And so loud, as they talked and laughed. He must be ever so careful. Everyone knew why the Star Men were so large. They ate children. All the kids knew that. They all had heard the terrible stories told by the oldest kids. That was why everyone hid from Star Men when they passed on the streets— you would be a fool not to.

He cautiously made his way to the incredible table. Squatting low, he quickly raised his arm and grabbed for a small brown thing on a plate at the edge. He was proud of his speed in snatching it. He put the food thing to his nose. It smelled incredibly good! His stomach rumbled so loudly that he feared the Star Men might hear. He knew the right thing to do would be to put this food into the bag he carried, but his hunger got the best of him as he shoved the bread roll into his mouth. Oh, he thought with wonder, it tasted even better than it smelled! He darted his arm up again and captured two more rolls which he did put into the bag. So easy! Again and again he snatched food. He would be a hero when he brought such an incredible haul back to the gang. This was a lucky day!

Suddenly something grabbed the back of his shirt and he was lifted up into the air! In terror, he thrashed about, but the great Star Man held him tightly. He was caught! His life was over. The Star Man turned him toward himself. His great teeth showed as he spoke in the Star Man language. Little Monkey closed his eyes, waiting for those terrible teeth to tear his flesh. When the bite did not come, he dared to crack open his eyes. Horror! Another even larger Star Man was before him. His teeth were even bigger! He was doomed. They were going to take turns eating him. He closed his eyes again tightly, stiffened in fear, waiting for the unbearable pain. The pain didn't come. Again he dared to open his eyes, but just a little.

"Hey, boy!" the Star Man bellowed.

Little Monkey squeezed his eyes shut and froze in terror.

"Relax! I don't bite!" the Star Man's voice bellowed more softly.

Oh, but you do! thought Little Monkey. *You also chew and you swallow!*

*

Dinner was laid out on the buffet. The officers served themselves generous portions, and then sat down to eat. They preferred eating in the kitchen, as it was very informal, and the cook (who was quite a comic) could join them. As they were enjoying their meal, Karl noticed a quick movement at the far end of the buffet table. What was it? He continued eating, but secretly kept watching. There! Again, another quick movement. Curious, Karl excused himself for a moment, got up, and walked away from the table. But instead of leaving, he made a quick detour behind the tall racks of kitchen supplies. He quietly made his way around the kitchen and came up behind the buffet table. There, crouched down, was a small boy. His thin tanned arm quickly darted up to the table and back again with his prize. Karl's soft boots made no sound as he came up behind the child. He grabbed the back of the startled kid's very dirty shirt and lifted him aloft.

"What have we here?" he said as he turned the thrashing boy toward himself.

One of the other officers came up to them, grinning widely. "What have you caught there, Karl, a little thief?"

"Hey, boy!" Karl spoke to his frightened catch in the boy's native language. "Relax, I don't bite!"

By that time, all the men from the table had joined them. Karl sat the child onto a nearby chair. He saw the boy tense up as if he were preparing to make a run for it, so he tightened his grip on his shirt. The group peered at the frightened boy.

"Look how thin he is!"

"I'll bet he hasn't eaten in a week."

Almost true, Little Monkey thought, *but I did eat a cooked rat yesterday.*

"Look how dirty he is," one of the other men said. "What are we going to do with him?"

Little Monkey looked fearfully from one great Star Man to another. Now they were talking in their strange language. He thought to himself, *if that one would loosen his hold just a tiny bit, maybe I could wiggle and get free. I still have my bag of food, so if I could just get loose ....* Unfortunately, the big Star Man did not loosen his grip. They peered at him like he was some pitiful creature, or more likely, a future meal. Then they spoke to him in his own language.

"Boy, what is your name?" one asked.

"How old are you?" asked another.

"Looks about 9 or 10. What are you doing here?"

"Isn't it obvious?" the Star Man who held him tightly said to the other. "He's hungry." Then he looked at the boy. "Are you hungry?"

Little Monkey dared to nod his head.

"So, you *do* understand. OK then, let's take care of that."

To Little Monkey's unbelieving eyes, the men dragged a small tray table before him. The others got plates and heaped them with food. They put the plates on the little table. They handed him eating utensils. Was this real? Were they offering him food—free

4

food? No, there must be another reason. Yes! They were fattening him up for their future meal! Of course! That had to be it. But his mind worked quickly and reasoned: He was starving. Here was food before him. The Star Men intended for him to eat. It smelled so good! They may indeed be fattening him up, but for now, why not eat? He was captured, for sure, but he may yet escape so he would need his strength. Truth be told, his empty stomach would have won any mental argument.

It had been a long time since he had seen the metal eating sticks, but he still tried to use them. The food kept sliding off, so in frustration and unbearable hunger, he dropped the eating stick and grabbed food with both hands and shoved it into his mouth. The Star Men laughed, but he didn't care. All he cared about in that moment was the delicious food. After he had eaten everything on the plate, and then licked it clean, the men gave him a glass of liquid. It looked like dirty water but it was so good! It was sweet. He gulped it down and bravely held the glass up for more. The Star Men laughed again as they re-filled the glass.

*

The officers watched the famished boy gobble food quicker than a garbage disposal. Even though his hands were filthy, they did not interfere as he dropped the spoon and began shoving food into his mouth. He drank iced tea like he had never had such a thing before. When he had eaten everything on his plate and licked clean the remaining smears of food, they gave him a warm wet towel and showed him how to wipe his mouth and hands.

The men rolled chairs over and surrounded the boy. Little Monkey knew he could not run at this time, as he was totally surrounded, so with his stomach full he relaxed a little—but just a little. He studied the Star Men. When they smiled at him, their teeth did not seem quite so terrifying.

Then questions began again: "What is your name? Where is your family? Where do you live?"

Little Monkey remained silent until one Star Man said, "He needs to go to the orphanage."

"No!" the boy spoke for the first time.

"So, you *can* speak!" The Star Man they called Karl boomed. "Why don't you want to go to the orphanage?"

Little Monkey looked from one face to another of the big men surrounding him. Since they had fed him, he figured he could talk to them until, of course, until they ate him. "I lived there when I was little."

"When you were little!" Karl laughed, then realized he might be insulting the child, so he continued, "You must have been very young then."

"Yes, I was. I was just a kid."

"What happened?" Karl asked with a softer voice.

Little Monkey took another drink of iced tea from the third filling of his glass, and continued, "I was there until the boss men came to take me to the basement to do mean things to me. I didn't want to go with them, so I ran away."

"What kind of mean things?" Karl asked, concerned.

The boy's wide eyes looked nervously from one big man to another, "I shouldn't talk about it, because they might find me and ... I can't tell you."

Karl decided not to press the issue, and instead changed the subject, "Where have you been living after you ran away from the orphanage?"

"I live with the gang."

"The gang? Who is in this gang?"

Little Monkey did not want to give too much information which could possibly be used to betray them, so he was vague, "Just a bunch of kids."

The men sat quietly around the small, thin, and very dirty child. The boy's big dark eyes still showed some fear, but at least he was not attempting to run.

"Where do you all live?"

The boy shrugged, "Any place we can find that's safe from the rain ... and other things."

*

What now? Little Monkey was wondering. Will they put me in a closet like they did at the orphanage? Would they give me more food before they eat me (as he knew they surely would) to fatten me up? He looked from one man to another and finally got the courage to ask the dreaded question: "When—are you going to—eat me?"

He was surprised as the big men actually looked startled.

"EAT you!" Star Man Karl exclaimed. "EAT YOU?" he incredulously repeated. "Whatever makes you think that we would *eat* you?"

"Not much of a meal, if you ask me," one of the men laughed.

Karl frowned at the man and then turned back to the boy. "Why ... why would you say that?"

Little Monkey was bewildered, but gathered his courage and said, "Everyone knows that the Star People eat children, that's why they're so big ...." His voice failed as several of the Star Men began laughing. He was frightened at their loud laughter, and also confused by it.

"Boy, listen to me," Star Man Karl said seriously. "You have nothing to fear. You have been told wrongly. Star People do NOT eat children. We don't eat anybody. Do you understand? We are tall because that is the way we are. We are from a different world than this one, that's all."

Little Monkey wanted to believe them. Could it be true? They had not made any move to harm him, but the stories ... they were so terrible. Then he reasoned: They had fed him—wonderfully fed him. He was not harmed. He did not seem in danger of being harmed in the near future. He had never heard that the Star Men were liars ... only eaters. He decided. He would wait and see ... as if he had any other choice. After all, he was still a captive.

*

The men moved their rolling chairs back to the comfort of their dining table. The cook brought them hot drinks in mugs. They sat the boy onto one of the chairs, but his head barely cleared the table top. So, they flipped the chair over, and adjusted the height all the way up. It was not perfect, but it was much better. The boy climbed up into it, still clutching his grimy food bag.

"What's the bag for?" Star Man Karl asked.

The boy looked guiltily from one man to another, "It's for food—for the gang."

"So, you were stealing food for the other kids, right?"

The boy nodded. "They're very hungry, like me ... but I'm not hungry now, but they still are," he rambled.

"Where are they?" another asked.

Again worried for their safety, he was vague in his answer, "Out there. Out back somewhere."

"Are they all young like you?"

"I'm the youngest and smallest ... but I'm quick ... and I can climb high. That's why they call me 'Little Monkey.'"

"Little Monkey!" The Star Men tried to hide their amusement. "Do you have any other name?"

"No," the boy paused, "just 'Little Monkey.' I don't remember anyone calling me anything else."

"So, they make you do the stealing?" Karl raised an eyebrow.

"Yes, because I'm the best at it."

No, Karl thought to himself, *it's because they were afraid and they talked you into it.* He felt a measure of respect for the small

8

boy's obvious bravery. "We didn't know there were any children still living on the streets. Since the orphanage was established, we thought that all had been found."

"Oh, there are lots of gangs. We hide when we see the Star People ... because, you know, they would catch us and eat us ..." Little Monkey's voice trailed off in embarrassment.

"Are your friends still waiting outside for you to bring them food?" a Star Man asked.

The boy nodded.

"We've got to do something. Those kids are starving," another Star Man said.

"I have an idea," the Star Man in a white apron interrupted. "How about we set out some food for your friends? Will they come get it if no one is around?"

"Yes," the boy assured him. "If no one can see them, you bet they will."

*

So, the cook set out a huge tray of food on an old table between the dumpster and the back steps. He began to open the dumpster, but then pretended that he forgot something, so he left the tray where it was and went back into the kitchen. He closed the door and turned off the outside light, as if finished at the kitchen door for the evening.

Little Monkey did not know what to think. The dreaded Star Men had not only fed him, but were now going to feed the other kids too!

*

The men talked together while they finished their hot drinks. Karl noticed that the boy looked uncomfortable as he squirmed in his chair. "Boy, do you have to go to the toilet?"

Remembering what a toilet was from his time spent at the orphanage, Little Monkey nodded anxiously.

9

"Come." Karl led the child to a washroom off the kitchen and waited ... he could hear the boy going ... and going. He chuckled to himself. The never-ending pee! After three glasses of iced tea, it was no wonder.

As they were about to leave the bathroom, Karl decided to educate the child. "We always wash our hands after using the bathroom ... here, let me show you." Karl led the boy to the sink, turned on the warm water, and squirted some soap into the boy's open palms.

Little Monkey smelled the enticing smell of the soap and attempted to taste it.

"No! Not food."

The boy jumped, startled by the big man's quick warning. Still though, he sniffed at it again and looked up at the Star Man.

"Alright, go ahead and taste it then, but I'm telling you, it is *not* food!"

The boy's tongue darted out to the sweet smelling soap in his hands, but then he quickly sputtered and spit.

Karl laughed, "See, I told you, it's NOT food!" He paused and then said, "Boy, look at me."

Little Monkey looked up at him.

"I tell you this. I will never lie to you." He waited a moment, "Do you understand?"

The boy looked into the great man's eyes and saw no malice. He nodded.

When they returned to the table, the men talked of what to do with the boy. They spoke in their own language, almost like he wasn't even there. He watched the Star Men as they talked among themselves. They were very tall to be sure, fully a head— maybe more—taller than the tallest men of his people, and Star Man Karl was one of the tallest of them all. But, as he looked at them, he realized that they were not *really* giants—not like giants of scary stories, not that kind of giant at all.

Their teeth were big, but as he studied their smiling faces, not really any larger than they should be. Maybe because their teeth were so very white, it made them appear larger than they actually were. Also, he noticed that their teeth were not sharp and pointed as he had always believed. The men were loud, but with clarity of reasoning far more mature for his age the boy realized that their loudness was born of confidence, not of a desire to be mean or frightening.

They wore clothing that looked the same as each other, but there were no torn places at all. Except for the Star Man Cook—he wore white with an apron that was smeared with food. And they all had boots—very fine boots. He looked at their hands, faces, and clothes. They were so clean! These Star People even *smelled* clean!

Star Man Cook brought him something that was covered with white powder and said, "Taste it." Even though he was still quite full, it smelled wonderful so he eagerly bit into it. As he did, some white cream squirted out the other side. The cook laughed. The boy eagerly licked it and sucked out more. It was so delicious! By the time he had finished, his face was a mess. With a large finger, Star Man Karl wiped a bit of cream filling off the boy's chin and playfully tapped it onto the end of his nose! It was the first time the Star Man had actually touched him, other than when he had caught him. But, he wasn't afraid anymore. The stories about the Star People had to be all wrong.

As the men talked on, the boy wildly scratched his head, leaving his oily matted dark hair sticking up strangely. The cook said one word: "Lice." All the Star Men instinctively leaned away from the scratching boy. The child's hands were clean, but it was obviously apparent that the rest of him was still extremely filthy.

11

He needed a bath.

It was decided. They would keep the child with them until tomorrow, and then decide what would be best for him. Karl spoke to the cook, who left and soon returned with lice shampoo.

*

Karl led the boy to the elevator. The child evidently had been in one before as he did not seem distressed. They rode up several floors. Karl explained to the boy about the bathtub and what was going to happen in it. They walked quietly down the carpeted hallway, passing many doors, and then stopped at one. "These are my quarters," Karl said as he opened the door. They walked through the living room to the bedroom, and then into the bathroom.

Karl filled the tub. He asked the boy to take off his clothes so he could get into the water. The child seemed anxious, so he left the bathroom until he heard the boy get into the tub.

"May I come in now?" Star Man Karl asked.

After a moment, the child answered, "OK."

The boy sat in the tub—with his filthy clothes still on. Karl couldn't help but chuckle, as he softly tried to explain why the boy needed to take *off* his clothes in order to clean himself. The child listened as he also explained how to use the soap and the wash cloth. Karl moved away and the boy watched him with suspicion as he gradually removed his ragged clothing.

Karl continued to talk softly to ease the child's fears. He encouraged and praised the boy's efforts to bath. He explained about the lice shampoo. The boy nervously let the big man wash his hair with the smelly bug shampoo, and then again with good smelling shampoo. Karl noticed, thankfully, that the child did have the circular marks on both arms showing that he had gotten the plague vaccine at some point.

When they were done, the water was dark with years of filth and who knows what else. Karl emptied the tub. The boy, no longer fearful, seemed entertained by the water swirling and glugging down the drain. Karl filled the tub again. The boy held his hands up under the warm water coming out of the faucet. He ended up squirting both himself and Karl!

Little Monkey was appalled! He had shot water at a Star Man! But instead of hitting him, the big man was laughing. He was actually *laughing*! At that moment he knew he could trust Star Man Karl, and so he dared to laugh too.

After the boy was washed a second time, Karl wrapped him in a large fluffy white towel and lifted him out of the tub. Little Monkey watched Star Man Karl as he opened drawers, and finally pull out a shirt that the Star Men wore under their uniforms. It didn't even have any holes, except for the proper arm and head holes, of course. It was white and soft—and felt good on his freshly scrubbed skin. They walked on the soft carpet over to a real bed—a gigantic bed. Karl held up the sheets for the boy to slip under.

"This is where you will sleep. I'll be in the next room. OK?"

The boy nodded.

The big man turned off the light and left, partially closing the door. Little Monkey peered about the room dimly lit by the light coming through the crack of the door. He was alone, but he felt safe. He touched the sheets around him ... so smooth and they smelled so nice. Everything about the Star People smelled nice. Just in case, he held up the sheet and looked under it. No ... nothing crawling. You should always check—everyone knows that.

Chapter 2

I'm All New!

Karl called softly to the sleeping boy. He hated to wake him as it was probably the first real sleep the poor child had in a long time. Suddenly the boy jumped and scurried fearfully to the far side of the bed.

"It's OK! Don't you remember? You're safe here."

Then Little Monkey *did* remember. So it wasn't a most wonderful dream—it was real!

"We need to get moving. Breakfast will stop being served soon."

Breakfast! Food! He was wide awake now. Still wearing the Star Man's undershirt, they rode the elevator down and walked to the kitchen. The wonderful smell of food almost overwhelmed him again. They went to the end of the big long table and he was handed a plate. So much food on the table, just like last night! When Star Man Karl asked if he wanted some of each dish, he always nodded eagerly, even though he didn't know what most of the food was. When they sat down, his plate was piled higher than each of the Star Men's plates!

As they ate, the discussion turned to the boy. "He needs to be checked out by the Doc."

"He can't stay here forever," another said.

The cook joined them at the table, glancing at the child. "This boy can't go around in Karl's underwear. You should go to storage and get him something that fits."

"You'll need to tell the High Commander about him."

Karl listened as he ate and finally said, "I'll take care of it—all of it."

The cook then said to the boy, "I'm going to set out another tray of food this morning. Do you think your friends will see it?"

"Yes," the boy mumbled with a mouth full of food. "They will."

After breakfast, Karl left to make some calls while the boy stayed with the cook as he cleaned up the kitchen. Star Man Cook told the boy that the tray of food that they had put out last night had been licked clean.

"Shall we make another?" He smiled at the small boy.

Little Monkey helped the cook fill another tray with breakfast. He was pleased that the Star Men were giving food to the gang. These Star People were nothing like what he had always believed before.

* * *

As they walked a couple of blocks down the street to the clinic, Karl explained what the doctor would do, and to not be afraid. When they arrived at the doctor's office, Karl lifted the boy up onto the examination table. Everything was so strange—and white. Karl saw the boy's eyes fill with fear when the doctor entered.

Little Monkey drew in his breath sharply. This "Doc" had white hair and was dressed all in white. He looked very scary—even scarier than any other Star Man he had ever seen.

Karl put his hand on the boy's shoulder and reassured him, "I'm right here and I am not leaving you. Don't worry, old Doc is not such a bad guy."

"Well, how are we today?" The all-white Star Man Doc said. "What is your name, son?"

The boy remained silent, but when nudged by Karl, he barely spoke, "Little Monkey."

"Little Monkey!" the doctor looked with amusement from the child to Karl. "So, Little Monkey, let's get you into the Medical Analyzer machine."

"No!" Karl said sharply, then more softly, "No."

The doctor looked at the anxious child and said, "OK then, we'll do this the old fashioned way."

Little Monkey watched the big white Star Man warily.

"So, may I listen to your heart?"

Sudden fear raced through him. *He's going to cut me open to get to my heart!*

Seeing the panic, Karl said, "Doc, maybe you should show him what that means. Listen to my heart, so the boy can see."

No! No! Thought Little Monkey. Surprised that he cared, he did not want nice Star Man Karl to be hurt. Watching with anticipated horror, the doctor put two things in his ears and put the other end of it on Karl's chest.

"See, it doesn't hurt. The doctor can hear my heart with this thing, that's all."

After that, the examination went fairly well. He didn't like the wood stick put into his wide-open mouth, but he actually enjoyed being weighed. He found that if he jumped a bit, the numbers on the scale changed.

The men were very patient.

*

When they left the doctor's office, Star Man Karl said, "Come on, boy, let's get you some decent clothes."

He followed the big man through the building and out the front. They walked back to the Star Man place, but instead of going inside, they turned toward a Star People flying car thing. He dared to ask, "Are we going to ride in that?"

"Sure," Karl said.

"Are we going to ride like a car, or ... fly?"

"Well, we could ride on the road with the wheels, but we can go much faster if we fly." He looked down at the boy, "You're not afraid, are you?"

Little Monkey gulped and answered, "I hope not."

Karl burst out laughing. His loudness did not frighten Little Monkey anymore. He even liked it now. It made him feel safe.

Karl opened the door of the flyer. The boy climbed in and sat in the seat—his legs stuck straight out because it was so big. Karl walked around and got into the pilot's seat. He operated some controls and then the flyer soundlessly lifted off the pavement. Up and up they went. Little Monkey held tightly to the edges of the much-too-large seat. His wide brown eyes stared down through the clear "bubble" surrounding the craft as the tree tops whizzed past below them.

"You OK?" Karl asked as he glanced sideways at the boy.

Little Monkey nodded, even though in truth, he wasn't quite sure ... and his full stomach wasn't quite sure either. Then the tree tops were gone and they were over a large area, with many huge metal things lined up in rows. "Are those airplanes?" he asked.

"Why, yes! Do you understand about airplanes?"

"Not really, I just know that they're supposed to fly in the air, just like we are."

"Well, not exactly like we are," Karl smiled, "but you have the right idea. They don't fly anymore—not since the plague—no one left to pilot them. Ah, here we are."

The flyer landed gently in a large parking lot—which had no cars. With mixed feelings of adventure and thankfulness that they had not crashed to the ground, the boy opened the door and climbed out of the craft. They walked up to a huge warehouse, with their footsteps echoing across the vast emptiness. Karl unlatched the heavy door and pushed it open. The boy stood in the doorway while Karl entered the darkness inside. Several minutes went by, and he began to wonder where Star Man Karl had gone. Suddenly, the lights came on.

"Wow!" the boy exclaimed, almost unbelieving his very eyes. There were, as it seemed, miles and miles of racks and shelves, all full of valuable stuff!

Karl, reading the signs on the high walls, led them to a section of clothing for children. They walked down an aisle, and stopped at a rack of shirts. He took a red one off the rail and held it up to the boy's chest. "Looks about right. Let's try it on."

The boy eagerly pulled off the huge undershirt he was still wearing as Karl prepared to slip the new shirt over his head. It had tags! All these clothes had tags! Tags meant that they were all brand new. He had never had anything actually *new* before, not ever.

Grinning at the boy's joy, Karl said, "Pick ten or so shirts from this section, and I'll be right back."

Little Monkey was so overwhelmed with his good fortune, he did not even notice when Karl returned with a shopping cart. Upon it Karl loaded about twenty brightly colored shirts from the boy's heavily laden arms. He wondered if the boy could count. Then they moved to another rack—one that had pants. They found the size that fit best, and together they picked jeans and shorts. Shoes were next. Little Monkey kicked off the ridiculously huge flip-flops that Karl had cut half the length off of, and sat in a chair. Finding the proper size took a little more time.

Karl led the boy to a full length mirror. Little Monkey could hardly believe it as he looked at himself. There he stood with a new shirt, new pants and new shoes.

"I am all new!" he exclaimed out loud.

Karl chuckled. Then, something off in the distance caught the boy's eyes. Toys! He remembered toys from the orphanage.

Karl, seeing the boy stare in fascination, said, "OK, let's go check that out."

Little Monkey almost felt faint. Toys! In boxes, in bags, and just out in the open on the shelves for the taking. Then he saw it. A red and black Super Rider! He ran to it, and stood in awe of such a thing. He dared to touch the handlebars.

Laughing, Karl said, "Go ahead. Try it out."

Little Monkey eagerly sat down in the seat. He put his feet on the pedals of the big front wheel. Karl stepped back and motioned for him to ride. And ride he did! He rode up and down the aisle. He felt like a King!

Karl motioned for him to come back. "You can ride all over the warehouse, but don't leave the building. I'm going to collect more things for you." Little Monkey grinned and nodded, and off he went.

Karl could hear the boy racing through the building, hollering with joy. He smiled, remembering his own childhood. He collected other items such as underwear, socks, jackets, and such. This warehouse was one of many that they had stocked with clothing collected from businesses in towns where the plague had been the worst ... all those clothes—but no one left to wear them.

The smooth floor of the warehouse was perfect for speed. Little Monkey raced up and down aisle after aisle. He careened around corners. He would brake suddenly and skid, spinning around. He was even able to make some "donut" circles. What great fun it was! It was the most fun he had ever had in his whole life. Ever!

*

When they returned to the Star Man's place, Little Monkey couldn't believe his ears when Star Man Karl said they were going to lunch. Another meal? Did this mean that these people ate three times a day? Then he remembered. They did eat several times each day at the orphanage ... but it was nothing like this!

Together they walked to the kitchen, where most of the Star Men were already eating. Little Monkey grinned happily at all the attention. They had him turn in circles while everyone admired his new clothes. Then he and Karl walked to the buffet table and filled their plates. After they were seated at the table and had started eating, the most amazing thing happened. In walked a Star *Woman*! Little Monkey had never seen one up close before. He stared, not even taking a bite of his sandwich.

"Commander, please excuse the intrusion," she said as she stiffly saluted Star Man Karl.

"At ease, Senior Airman, you must be new here. What's up?"

The woman relaxed her posture and handed him a card. Karl pressed the card with his thumb and read the message that appeared on it. "Thank you, you may go." He smiled at the woman and then added, "We're a bit more relaxed here than you are probably used to."

"Yes, sir," she smiled as she glanced around the highly unsuitable kitchen dining arrangement, complete with a small ragged-haired native boy sitting among the men. "I can see that."

When she left, the men rolled their eyes and made comments in their language that Little Monkey did not understand. They all were grinning and laughing, so he guessed it was because she was quite beautiful.

20

"Get a grip, guys," Commander Karl laughed with them. "Obviously, another ship has arrived."

"Yeah, we haven't seen HER before! I hope there are plenty more just like her!" Star Man Cook hooted.

"Show some respect, gentlemen," Karl smiled as he got up. "Gio," he said to the cook as he held up the card. "Can I leave the boy in your care while I take care of this?"

"Sure! Don't worry. He can be my official helper."

The boy looked from Commander Karl to Cook Gio. He smiled. He liked Cook Gio almost as much as he liked Commander Karl.

*

After several hours, Karl returned to find Gio giving the boy a ride on his shoulders. Little Monkey exclaimed, "Look how high I am! I could touch the ceiling!"

"Time to get back to work," Gio said as he turned to go through the doorway.

Karl quickly pulled the boy off Gio's shoulders. "You can't go through the door; he won't clear it and you'll knock him cuckoo."

Little Monkey giggled at the very idea.

*

After dinner, many of the officers gathered outside and sat around the biggest bathtub Little Monkey had ever seen. They called it a pool. As they sat and talked, they kept glancing up at the stars. Then the show started—bright streaks of light raced across the night sky!

Commander Karl explained, "Those bright lights are actually pieces of rock traveling through space, and when they enter your planet's atmosphere—the air—they burn up and look just like that."

After a while, fewer and fewer of the bright lights shot across the sky, and one by one the other Star Men left. Finally it was just the two of them looking up at the brilliant stars shining above them in the darkness.

Little Monkey asked, "Which star did you live on?"

Karl smiled. "We can't see it from here. Actually, we don't live on a star. Each one of those stars is a *sun*, just like the sun here. My people come from a *planet* that revolves—goes around—the sun, just like yours does. My planet is very old," he mused, "but we think yours is fairly young. You see, we are explorers. Our people have traveled to many, many worlds."

Little Monkey listened intently.

"Most are just big rocks, but some have life—mostly simple life, and much different from ours. When we found your world, we were shocked. It was so much like ours that we couldn't believe it. The atmosphere, the climate, the mineral composition, plant and animal life, most everything. Even the people!" He put his muscular arm next to the child's thin one and gently squeezed the two together. "We are of the same genetic ... we are made of the same stuff. It's amazing!"

Little Monkey looked at him in awe.

"As soon as our people arrived here, they quickly realized there was a terrible problem. The plague. Most of the entire planet's population was either dead or dying. Our people were torn. They were not supposed to interfere with any life forms they encountered. Yet, how could they stand by and watch the inhabitants here die? Our people on that first ship had to make a choice: obey standard orders or help. They were undecided until one of them said that if the situation were reversed, and it was *our* planet, would we want aliens to help us or just stand by and watch us die? That decided it. They would do all they could to help.

"So, they developed a vaccine and gave it to every person they found. It was tedious and took time. Unfortunately, some entire continents were ... without survivors. They concentrated on the largest populations. Some were afraid of us, because we were so much bigger than they were," he winked at the boy, "but being so sick, most didn't much care. Many of the sickest people ... it was sadly too late for us to help them. But the others, after they got the vaccine and recovered, also helped us with the rescue operations.

"So many people had died ... and unfortunately, their skills died with them, so we had to rebuild the infrastructure. We got power and water back on. We got farms operating again. Much has been accomplished, but more still needs to be done. Here it is, five years and many ships later, and we are still finding pockets of people hiding from the disease, but still getting it. It's a big world, and we are but a few. Do you understand what I have told you?"

"Yes," the boy said sadly. "I do understand. I've seen sick people. They had blood coming out of their eyes and nose, and everywhere. One time it made me throw up."

"I'm sorry you had to see that," Karl said gently, and then changed the subject. "I just arrived here about six months ago. We decided to live here ..." he motioned behind him, "in this hotel. It was unoccupied and much better than field barracks, plus it's more convenient than having to go to and from the ship everyday. We did have to make some modifications though; we brought beds that fit us. Our feet stuck out of the beds here!"

Both he and the boy laughed.

"The trip took two months from home to here, and I spent most of it learning *your* language." He chuckled, as he tussled the boy's hair. "Your world has several languages, and yours is one of the harder ones!"

"No, it's easy." the boy disagreed. "You just ... talk."

"You *think* it's easy because you're used to it. Try to learn mine and you'll see what I mean!"

23

"I want to!" exclaimed the boy.

"You want to what?"

"I want to learn the Star language. I want to!"

*

So, language lessons began. Karl would say the name of an object in his language and the boy would repeat it. Then, as review, Karl would make up a sentence, such as "I'm sitting down on a ...," and the boy would fill in the word *chair*, but in the Star Man's language. It became a great game, and Little Monkey was a very quick student. Soon all the Star Men were teaching him, and he learned much. Several days later, Little Monkey surprised Karl with a complete perfect sentence, without any coaching from anyone.

* * *

It was a sunny afternoon, and Commander Karl was off duty ... sort of. Since he was in charge of Sector Seven, he was really *on* duty all the time, but he had times when he did what he wanted, and this day he wanted to go for a swim. Little Monkey was somewhat hesitant to join him.

"Do you know how to swim?" Karl asked as he walked down the steps into the water.

"I don't know. I never did it before, I think."

"Come on then, let's give it a try. Don't be afraid, I'm right here."

Little Monkey clung to the rail and gingerly stepped down one step at a time into the pool. The water was nicely cool against his warm body. He stepped off the last step. The water came up to his chest.

"It gets deeper the farther in you go," Karl said, "so let's stay here in the shallow end for a while."

Karl asked the boy to try to swim from there to the side of the pool without touching the bottom. He tried, but just thrashed about, going nowhere. Then Karl told the boy to stay there and he would show him how to swim.

Karl pushed himself off into the deep end. His strong muscular arms cut effortlessly through the water as he swam from one side of the pool to the other. He returned to the boy. Sparkling water droplets dripped from his dark hair onto his nicely tanned skin. "Did you see? You use your arms to pull the water and you use your feet to kick it away."

Karl had the boy hold onto the side of the pool and practice kicking. His skinny little legs did the best they could. He then held the boy up with one strong hand on his belly, and had him try to use his arms and legs at the same time. The boy seemed to be getting the idea, but Karl did not let go. He wanted the boy to go solo only when he was ready—and chose to do it. He also tried to teach the boy how to float, but Little Monkey was a bit fearful to put his head back so far into the water. Knowing they had plenty of time to visit the pool all summer, they spent the rest of the lesson squirting water at each other with their hands, and then sunning themselves at the poolside.

*

The next day Karl took Little Monkey to the gym.

"We want to look good for the ladies, right?" Karl winked at the boy as they walked down the steps to the gymnasium.

"Why?" Little Monkey asked.

"I'm just joking around," Karl smiled. "We need to keep strong and in shape ... never know what to expect in this job."

The gym was in the basement level of the hotel. Several other Star Men were there—he knew some of them from meal times. They were on strange machines, going up and down, or back and forth ... and they were all sweaty. For the first time, he was with Star People who *didn't* smell very good.

Karl explained what they were doing. Then he arranged something on the back of one of the metal machines, and lay back upon the reclined workout bench in front of it. He pulled on two handles, and some heavy looking blocks lifted up.

The boy watched with fascination as Karl's muscles bulged each time he pulled the handles. "I want to be strong like you!"

"And you will be," Karl smiled at him. "You want to try this one out?"

Karl got up and set the machine on the lowest setting. The boy lay back on the bench and Karl put the handles into his small hands.

"Now pull!"

Little Monkey pulled on the handles and the weights came up easily.

"That's too easy for you. Let's try the next setting."

When it was set, the boy pulled on the handles, and the weights didn't come up quite as quickly. "That's hard!" he exclaimed.

"That's good!" Karl laughed. "Try some more if you like."

The boy pulled six times more and then sat up. "It's your turn now."

So, Karl smiled as he re-set the weights and continued his exercise. Some of the other men around suggested various exercises for the boy. They had him lift metal things that had "5" stamped onto them. They had him tuck his toes under a bar at the end of a workout bench, and then he rose up and then back down—like sitting and lying down. Two of the men held up a metal bar for him to try to lift himself up using only his hands and arms. That was really hard! Then he sat on a bench of a machine (which the men adjusted) and put his feet on the pedals and pushed. That was the easiest thing to do in the gym ... until they added more weight to it.

When Karl was done, Little Monkey was sweaty just like the others, but he was happy. He was one of the group, all making their muscles strong together! Then Karl suggested a swim before dinner.

It was a perfect day!

Chapter 3

The Basement

The Star Men were concerned with the situation of the street kids. They needed food and shelter—and they needed an education. They were appalled that they had not seen the kids before, who were obviously very skillful in hiding from them. They asked Little Monkey if he would try to convince the kids of his gang to accept help. The boy agreed.

Before dinner that evening, Little Monkey sat out back on the kitchen steps—waiting to hear the call. Shortly it came—the special call that sounded like a bird ... sort of. He returned the call. One by one the street kids in his gang came out of hiding.

"Is that you Li'l Monk?"

"Yeah, it's me."

"You're not dead?"

"No, of course not."

"They didn't eat you?"

"No." He held out his arms and with just a hint of sarcasm said, "See any teeth marks?"

"I don't get it. You should be dead, but here you are ... and you have new stuff!" The oldest boy looked him up and down. The other kids enviously stared wide-eyed at him.

"They gave me these clothes." He stretched his shirt out to show them. "*New* clothes—everything had tags!"

"Yeah? So what's going on here?" The oldest boy narrowed his eyes.

Little Monkey took a deep breath, "The Star People aren't like we thought. They're nice! They didn't hurt me; they gave me food ... and they've been giving *you* food too! They just want to help us—all of us."

"Are you ever stupid!" the leader scowled. "Star People want to eat us, we all know that. This is some kind of trick. They're pretending to be nice to you so they can catch us—like they caught you. And then it will be all over. We'll be their dinner for sure!"

Little Monkey felt a new kind of courage and confidence within himself as he contradicted the leader, "Look Jake, you're wrong." He looked at the others. "We were all wrong. The Star People really *are* nice."

He turned back to Jake. "It was my lucky day when they caught me. I'm glad they caught me! Like we always say: Don't look a gift horse in the mouth." (He wasn't quite sure what a gift horse was and why anyone would want to look into its mouth, but he knew that it meant something like: if anything good comes along, don't criticize or try to figure it out, just accept and enjoy it.)

"No," Jake said to the other kids. "It's a trap. Let's go before it's too late." He turned to leave, but the other kids hesitated. "NOW!" he barked. The kids, conditioned to Jake's leadership, glanced back at Little Monkey as they melted into the shadows and disappeared.

Disappointed, Little Monkey got off the steps and went back into the Star Man kitchen. Even though the plan didn't work like they had hoped it would, the cook continued to put out a tray of

food at each mealtime, and the food continued to disappear—
without even one single crumb left.

*

During the days that followed, Little Monkey stayed with Cook
Gio when Karl had to take care of official business elsewhere.
Otherwise, he stayed with Karl in his office. He sat at a table in the
corner and sometimes drew pictures on paper with colored
drawing sticks; and sometimes he looked at scenes of other
worlds on a viewer; and sometimes he made buildings out of
small toy blocks; but always, he tried to remain quiet.

He watched the Star People come and go. Most saluted
Commander Karl when they arrived and then again when they
left. New Star People had arrived in a ship recently. Since
Commander Karl was in charge there, they came to him for
assignments. They spoke in their language, and bit by bit, Little
Monkey learned to understand more and more of it.

It sounds boring, but it really wasn't.

Then one day, the same Star Lady that he had seen before
came to Karl's office.

"Thank you, Senior Airman," Commander Karl said as she
handed him official documents requiring his physical hand-written
signature.

As he read through the papers and signed them, she couldn't
help staring at him. He was so handsome! His dark wavy hair, his
strong square jaw, his broad shoulders, his uniform sleeves that
were almost too tight over his muscular arms ... and he looked
young, probably in his early thirties. She was startled and
embarrassed when he suddenly looked up to find her studying
him so intently.

"Thank you," he said smiling as he handed her the signed
forms. "You came in on the *Traveler*, right?"

"Yes, sir."

"How are you finding your new post here?"

She smiled, "Very nice, sir. Almost like home."

"Good then, we want everyone to feel welcome."

She saluted and turned to go. Now it was Karl's turn to study her as she walked away: her long golden brown hair pulled gently back off her face and falling down her back in waves, her small waist and feminine figure.

Little Monkey watched them both with curiosity, but he said nothing. Then, as she was about to go out the door, she gave Little Monkey a smile and a little wave of her hand. He looked into her eyes and saw the same kindness that he saw in Star Man Karl's eyes. He smiled and waved back.

*

Karl had informed the High Commander about the boy in their care. He had requested that the boy be allowed to stay with them for a few days. The High Commander agreed, but said that eventually the child should probably go to the local orphanage. He also agreed to let Commander Karl decide what was best.

So, Karl spoke to Little Monkey about his future. "Do you remember anything about your life before you went to the orphanage? Do you remember your parents? Your family?"

The boy shook his head. "I don't think so. I don't remember much from when I was at the orphanage either, except that I was scared sometimes. They put me in the closet when I was bad ... and sometimes they hit me. And sometimes, if they were really mad, they wouldn't let us eat. That was the worst ... well, not the very worst."

"What was the very worst?"

The boy glanced up at Karl and looked away. "I don't want to tell you, they told us not to tell."

"Why didn't they want you to tell?"

"They said it's a secret, so we didn't talk much about it, but sometimes we whispered. If the boss men heard us talking about the basement, we would get hit hard—very hard. Sometimes kids would run away. Jake, our gang leader, was at the orphanage and he ran away from it too."

Karl changed the subject, "We have to decide where you need to live. I see that you don't want to go back to the orphanage, and I don't blame you. Would you like to continue staying here, with us?"

Momentarily shocked at the very idea of returning to the orphanage, then immediately happy at the idea of staying with the nice Star People, he eagerly said, "Yes! I want to stay. I really like it here!"

"OK then," Karl said smiling, "but you need to go to school."

*

So, Little Monkey started his education. Karl brought him to school in the morning and picked him up in the afternoon—in a flyer! Driven by a Star Man! That gave the boy instant respect from the amazed school kids.

The school gave him homework. After dinner, when they all sat and talked, Little Monkey would bring it out. He didn't like homework, but it wasn't so bad because everyone helped him with it—even the Star Men who he didn't know very well. Little Monkey felt happy and at peace. They all cared about him. They genuinely cared, especially Star Man Karl. He thought back as far as he could remember ... no one had ever really cared about him before.

*

Many of the children at school were from the orphanage. Karl was bothered by what happened in the orphanage basement. Considering the hard lives children of this world have had to endure since the plague, he knew it was serious. He didn't think it was something "awful" as in having to clean one's room, as he would have thought when he was a child. Karl suspected abuse, but he needed to know for sure before he could take any action.

When they were alone, he unhappily decided to bring up the subject. "I know that you and your friends are afraid of the orphanage. You said that very bad things happened there. Would you tell me about it?"

Little Monkey stopped playing with the toy car in his hands. Without looking up, he said slowly, "Why do you want to know ... about that?"

"I want to know because an orphanage should be a good place, somewhere kids can go and live, and be safe. We have been supplying many orphanages for years, and we need to know if the people in charge of the children are doing right ... and if they aren't, I'm going to do something about it."

Little Monkey looked at Karl. What went on there was *not* right. Star Man Karl *is* a good man ... and he believed that Star Man Karl *would* do something about it. So, he took a deep breath and began. "I don't remember much from when I was there, but I do remember the bad boss men. We were all scared of them, even the biggest boys. At night, after we went to bed, the boss men came to take boys. When I heard them coming, I climbed up the bunk beds and jumped to the top of the tall bookcase and squished myself down, so they never could get to me. That's when the kids started calling me 'Little Monkey.'"

Karl interrupted, "Do you remember what they called you before 'Little Monkey'?"

He thought for a moment. "They called me 'kid,' I think. I don't remember anything else."

Karl said, "Go on."

"After a while, the boys would come back—sometimes they were crying. The boss men had sticks and they said if anyone

33

talked about it, they would hurt us real bad with the sticks and kill us. We were all so scared."

The boy paused, and Karl gently encouraged, "Go on."

"One time, I came from the bathroom and the boss men were already there. They grabbed me but I kicked and punched as hard as I could, and I got away and ran outside and I never went back."

Karl studied the uncomfortable boy, and then said, "You need to tell me what the boss men did to the kids they took to the basement."

The boy squirmed, and with his voice barely above a whisper he answered, "They took little black whips and they beat the boys with them, and they laughed when the boys cried, and they told them to be quiet or they would beat them harder. I think they did other bad things but I don't know what they were. When they brought the boys back from the basement, they made them and us promise not to tell or they would hurt us even more and kill us."

"This is awful," Karl said angrily.

The boy quickly looked up. "Are you mad at me?" he asked with big anxious eyes. "Was it our fault that they wanted to hurt us?"

"Mad at you? No. Never. Those bad things that those evil men did .... It was THEIR fault, not any of the boys' fault at all. Those scumbags that hurt those kids ..." Karl wanted to say what he thought of them, but not in front of the boy.

*

So, Karl devised a plan. Little Monkey agreed to try to get some of the boys from the orphanage to talk to him about the abuse. Since Little Monkey had lived there himself and knew all about it, he gained one boy's confidence and got the names of the boss men that the children feared so much. The boy said that the two bosses came almost every night, after "lights out," and took two boys to the basement. Karl needed proof, so he planned to catch the evil men in the act.

* * *

The two terrified boys walked down the narrow steps to the basement. At the end of the hallway was a dimly lit room. Behind them, the two bosses talked together as if they were taking a casual stroll. The boss men gruffly told the boys to go inside the room. Unhappily, they did as they were told, for if they did not then they would surely be beaten even harder.

Suddenly a great Star Man appeared! His face was red with rage! He grabbed each boss man by the front of their shirts. The Star Man's muscles bulged and the veins in his neck stood out as he lifted both of them up into the air and slammed them back against the wall. The boys, already terrified, were frozen with fear.

The great Star Man bellowed, "You pieces of ..." then, mindful of the two boys, he said, "filth! You perverts! You have been entrusted to take care of these kids, not abuse them!"

The two evil men—their eyes wide with surprise and fear— began to sputter their innocence.

"Shut up, swine!" He dropped them back down to the floor but kept a strong hold on their shirts, twisted in his mighty fists. Then the Star Man lowered his voice, and turned to the terrified boys, "It's OK, you are not going to be hurt ... I will not hurt you." He turned to the two wriggling in his grasp and moved close to their frightened faces. "And," he growled between clinched teeth, "these two maggots are not going to hurt you either, EVER AGAIN!"

He turned back to the trembling boys, "Kids, go on ... go back to your rooms."

The boys, still in terror, did not move.

"Go on," the Star Man said more softly. "Go ahead and go back. Really, it's OK," he nodded to them reassuringly. "Really. You can go."

The boys were nearly unbelieving the turn of events. With cautious looks darting between the hated bosses and the fearsome Star Man, they edged past the men and ran for their lives.

With the boys out of hearing, Karl bellowed and snarled exactly what he thought of the two in his grasp, using words he had never used before from his own language. Even though the two evil men probably did not understand all the words, they certainly understood their intent. Karl wanted to beat the snot out of them, but because he was so angry, he was afraid that he might kill them. After a while and with most of his immediate rage spent, he jerked each of them upward. "Do you want to walk or should I just drag your worthless hides?"

When they got upstairs, Karl threw his prisoners to the floor. By then, several other Star Men were there, and then the local police arrived. While the Star Men had no official authority, the police always deferred to their judgment. The officers "cuffed" the two and took them away, with a promise from Karl to soon go to the police station and make a formal complaint.

Several days later after the police had investigated the proceedings at the orphanage, Karl got an appointment to speak with the city council which the Star People had helped to establish. Along with city services, they were trying to get the local social systems back up, just as the people had before the plague. After all, the Star People were there to help, not take over. The city council, horrified at what had been going on, agreed to immediately get new administrators for the orphanage and have permanent and consistent oversight thereafter. Karl was pleased and felt very good about righting a terrible wrong.

Before dinner time, Little Monkey again sat on the steps outside the back door of the kitchen. He waited for the bird call signal. Soon it came and he answered it back. Jake appeared first, then about eight other kids slipped out of the shadows.

"Hey, Li'l Monk, you're still alive, I see."

"Of course," Little Monkey said matter-of-factly. "I told you they don't eat kids. That's just stupid."

"Are they going to bring out food tonight?" one of the other kids asked.

"I'll do the talking!" Jake interrupted.

Little Monkey answered the child, "Yes, they are, but I wanted to come out here first and talk to you ... to all of you."

"Well, what?" Jake asked impatiently.

"The Star People want to help you. They want to help all the kids on the street. They want to take you all to the orphanage where ...."

Jake interrupted, "The orphanage! Are you crazy? You were there! You know what happens there!"

Little Monkey held up his hands, "No, no, it's not like that anymore! Star Man Commander Karl took care of the bosses! He beat them up and sent them to jail. They're gone! It's OK there now."

"They got beat up?" Jake asked eagerly.

"Well, ... yeah," Little Monkey embellished the story some. "They were real messed up!"

Jake was pleased as he relished the idea of the bosses getting some payback.

Little Monkey continued, "You can't live on the streets forever. At the orphanage there is food—no rats! You can sleep in real beds inside—where it's warm in the winter and cool in the summer. You get medicine if you get sick, and you get new clothes!"

"They took our bus," one of the kids said sadly.

"What?" Little Monkey asked, puzzled.

"Yeah," Jake explained, "a few days ago when we got back there, a huge crane was lifting our bus up onto a big truck. It was awesome! But now we don't have it to live in anymore. So, we found another place closer to here—where the food is."

"Our new place isn't as good as the bus," another child said.

"Well, it seems like a perfect time to go to the orphanage! You need a better place. How about it?"

Jake was unsure as the other kids murmured that it just *might* be a good idea.

Little Monkey thought quickly. "How about this ... just you go, Jake, and talk to some of the kids who are there at the orphanage now. Then you can decide if what I'm telling you is true or not."

"Oh, I don't know about that," Jake hesitated. "Maybe ... maybe someone else should go."

"Come on, you're the leader of the gang, right? It should be *you* that goes! You're not afraid, are you?"

"No!"

"Good then, be here at lunch-time tomorrow and we'll go!"

"No," Jake mumbled. "I ... it's not a good idea."

"You *are* afraid, aren't you!"

"No!"

Remembering how Jake was, and the ways he used to get the other kids to do what he probably was too afraid to do himself, Little Monkey resorted to Jake's favorite tactic—something stupid that he absolutely hated, but decided he needed to try anyway. "I dare you!" he challenged. "I double dare you!"

"I'll be here!" Then Jake boasted, "I'm not afraid of anything!"

*

The next day, true to his word, Jake and the gang appeared at lunch and waited. Little Monkey joined them while they ate the sandwiches and drank the fruit drinks that Gio had put out.

"Commander Karl is going with us ... we're going in a flyer."

Jake's eyes got wide.

"It's fun! I ride in a flyer all the time. And Star Man Commander Karl is one of the nicest of all the Star People—he wouldn't hurt a fly!"

"What about the bosses?" Jake said with his mouth full. "Wasn't he the one who beat them up?"

"Yeah, but the bosses are much worse than flies!"

Then they both laughed. Jake almost choked on his sandwich. It was the first time he had laughed in a very long time.

When they had finished eating, Little Monkey went inside for a moment and then came right back out again. "Ready? Let's go!" He led Jake around the building to the front where Karl was already waiting in the flyer.

"Hi, Jake," the big man said softly. "Ready to go for a ride?"

The skinny teenager nodded fearfully.

Little Monkey opened the passenger door and had Jake sit in the back. He then sat proudly in the front seat, next to Karl. He was enjoying this ... he couldn't help it. Jake had always been so bossy to him.

As they lifted off, he turned around in his seat to look at Jake, who was pale as a ghost under the dirt on his grimy face. "Don't be scared."

"I'm not!" Jake lied.

They quickly arrived at the orphanage. Several children ran up to the fence surrounding the playground when they saw the flyer land. Jake got out and walked over to them while Little Monkey waited in the flyer. He wanted Jake to get the facts for himself, without any pressure from him. When Jake came back, he seemed mostly convinced. They flew back to the hotel, and then he and Jake rejoined the waiting kids. Jake told the others what he had heard, and they all agreed that they would go to the orphanage to live.

After about an hour had passed, the orphanage school bus came to pick them up. As they entered it, Jake threatened Little Monkey, "If this place is not like you said, we'll run away again. And I'll come for you!"

But Little Monkey wasn't worried—not one bit.

Chapter 4

Starship

After breakfast, the Star Men sat around discussing the other kids still living on the street. They would ask for help from the population to find the cleverly hiding kids, but that might not be enough. Convincing Little Monkey's gang to go to the safety of the orphanage was so successful that it gave Karl an idea. Perhaps having a *child* talk to the other street kids might be the key to helping them all. But, he needed to get permission from the High Commander in order to include a native boy in his plan.

As everyone was relaxing after finishing breakfast, Karl left the table to make a call. After a few minutes he returned, got another cup of a hot drink, sat down, and said to the group, "If the boy is to accompany us, I had to get the High Commander's 'OK.' I called for an appointment to see him, so he'll see us later this afternoon—on the ship." Karl looked at Little Monkey, "Want to take a trip to our starship?"

The boy's big brown eyes lit up! "Go to your starship? In outer space? Yes, sir! Wow!"

*

Karl picked up Little Monkey from school and they returned to the hotel where he had the boy wash his hands and face. When they were ready to leave, Karl ran a comb through the boy's dark hair, but as they walked to the flyer, a gentle breeze messed it all up again. Karl just smiled and shook his head as they entered the flyer.

"Are we going to the starship in this?"

"No," Karl answered. "Flyers are not pressurized—they're only for local travel. We'll be taking a 'transport.'"

In just a few minutes, they arrived at the Star People landing field. In a neat row, there stood several bright gleaming transport ships ... that looked like giant eggs—eggs that had been stretched longer! They left the flyer and walked up to one of the "eggs" where several men were talking. The boy was in awe as he looked up at the silvery metal ship. It towered above them. It was huge!

Karl said a few words to the men, and then together they climbed the steps to the big egg's opening above. When they got inside, they walked down the narrow way between short rows of deep blue seats. There were some people already sitting in the seats, and they nodded to Karl as he and the boy passed by them.

Karl stopped and motioned for the boy to enter a row next to a window. Little Monkey felt the soft fuzziness of the plush seat as he sat down. The rows of seats reminded him of a theater. He knew about a theater. There were no more movies, so the gang would sleep there. It was really dark, but the seats were soft to curl up on. It was a pretty good place until it burned down.

The ship was very, very quiet, except for soft music playing from somewhere far away, or so it seemed. Because it was so quiet, the boy whispered, "Is everyone here going to the starship?"

"You don't have to whisper, and yes, the transport is used mostly for trips to and from the ship."

"Does the starship have a name?"

"Yes, it's called (he said the name in his language). It means the *Seeker*. There are two other starships in orbit here, and they are the *Searcher* and the *Traveler*. The *Traveler* just arrived recently. They are above other parts of the planet, so we won't be able to see them from here. Since we're explorers, the ships have names that mean to look for, or to find things," Karl explained.

"Like when we looked for things—especially food—and took them?"

"No, not exactly. Stealing is wrong, but you and your friends took things to survive. Thankfully, that's all over now."

Several more Star People entered and sat down. The door closed and then a voice from somewhere said something. In a few seconds, they were pushed gently back into their seats as the ship lifted off the ground. The pressure increased some as their speed accelerated. It felt exciting!

"Quick, look out the viewport," Karl said.

The boy turned to the window next to him. The land below was shrinking away. The buildings got smaller, then the whole city shrank. The land changed from distinct areas to splotches of greens and browns. As the transport rose, the boy could see the curvature of his planet in the horizon. Suddenly the viewport turned dark and the surprised boy turned to Karl.

"The viewport goes dark automatically when we enter 'the roll,'" Karl explained. "You see, our ship here has to match the rotation of the starship. Sometimes the roll disorients some people if they happen to be looking at the land below." He smiled at the boy. "Don't want anyone getting sick in here!"

Then they felt the artificial gravity engage. Before the puzzled boy could ask, Karl explained. "Natural gravity is the force that makes your feet stay on the ground. When our much smaller ship enters space, we lose the natural gravity of the planet, so we have developed another type of artificial gravity that we can turn on when we need it ... it's to make everyone comfortable. Now, on the starship, we make gravity by rotating the hull. Do you know what would happen if there were no gravity at all?"

Confused, the boy shook his head.

"If there were no gravity, you would just float around, along with everything else. This drinking glass would float, those papers over there would float, and you and I would float—just float around in the air!"

Little Monkey laughed at the ridiculous idea. How silly! Star Man Karl had to be joking.

As they approached the starship, the viewport became clear again. Little Monkey jumped a bit in his seat when he saw the great spaceship. It was huge! He had never seen anything so big in his life! It looked like a big ... hotdog! With a big fat bun around it! We are in an egg going to a hotdog! He giggled in his thoughts. He wished he could tell the gang about this—they would never believe it.

Soon, the edges of the huge ship disappeared out of view as they moved closer and closer to the hull. Then they heard a soft thud. They had attached and were secured to the airlock. Everyone exited the transport into a metal room. Then they left that and walked down a carpeted hallway ... and walked and walked. There were many rooms off the hallway, but they went past them all and then stopped at an open door. They checked in with the secretary, and waited a few moments before entering the office beyond.

*

"Reporting as ordered, sir." Commander Karl snapped a smart salute. Not a split second after, the boy also executed a perfect salute.

Surprised, Karl glanced sideways at the boy.

The High Commander's eyebrows went up, then he gruffly said, "At ease, Commander."

Both Karl and the boy together smartly executed the "at ease" position.

A quick smile almost passed the High Commanders lips. "I assume this is the young man for the operation?"

"Yes, sir. His name is ... Little Monkey."

"Yes, I have that here in the request report. You both may sit down."

They sat in the large comfortable chairs, but the seat was so high that the boy's feet hung in the air above the floor.

The High Commander studied the boy and then leaned toward him. "Little Monkey, do you understand what the Commander has in mind for you? The operation to go to children living in the streets and try to convince them to get help?"

Following Karl's professional manner, he said stiffly, "Yes, sir, I want to do it. I want to help them. I... I used to be one of them."

"Very good then." The High Commander leaned back into his chair and continued studying the boy. "Commander, as long as you can assure me that every precaution will be taken for the child's safety, I will approve this."

"Yes, sir. I won't let anything happen to him. Ever."

The High Commander nodded. "Good. Dismissed!"

Karl stood and the boy quickly did as well. Together, the man and boy saluted in perfect unison, turned smartly, and left the office ... but not before Karl caught the High Commander's smile.

When the door closed behind them, Karl asked, "Where did you learn to salute like that?"

"I've been watching!" the boy replied, grinning.

"You have indeed!" Karl smiled. "You've been watching *very* well."

*

After they left the High Commander's office, Karl took the boy to the lounge. A huge viewscreen took up much of one wall.

"Wow! Outer space is really big!"

Karl chuckled, "Yes, it certainly is … look! Here comes the planet."

Fascinated, the boy watched his world travel from one side of the viewscreen to the other.

Karl explained, "It appears that the planet is the one moving, but it is really us—in this ship. We are the ones that are in a relatively slow spin … to make gravity, remember?"

The boy nodded, even though he still wasn't sure about this "gravity" thing.

"It's about dinner time," Karl said, looking down at the boy. "Want to eat here?"

Little Monkey nodded. He was always ready for food.

They left the lounge and walked down several more long hallways, and then entered through great double doors. Inside was a huge beautiful room—with fancy lights above, like a roof of stars! Lots of Star People were there, including many Star Ladies.

Then they turned and entered another room next to the magnificent dining area. It was a long room that was bustling with activity. Everyone stood in a line and people behind a counter dished food onto plates. Karl put two trays on the tray slide. Little Monkey's chin barely cleared it as he pushed his tray along. He looked around, as more Star People got in line behind him. They were all so tall and they didn't seem to look down much. He hoped no one would accidentally step on him.

Karl held up two fingers for two plates. Two plates, one person—the man behind the counter looked confused. Karl nodded downward toward the boy. The man leaned forward until he could see what Karl was referring to. Then he grinned broadly and set down two plates.

Karl spoke for the child as to what to put on his plate, because the boy could barely see above his tray. When they left the cafeteria line, Karl carried his tray with one strong hand, but the boy carefully took his with both hands. They walked toward a table near a big viewscreen showing millions of sparkling stars in the vast darkness of space.

As they passed tables, people looked with curiosity at the boy. Some recognized and called out to Karl. Suddenly, one of the cafeteria servers rushed past them carrying a tall stool. He swiftly removed a table chair and set the stool in its place. Karl thanked him and lifted the boy up onto it. Some Star People came to their table and greeted Karl in their language. Karl invited them to sit down and join them.

As Karl removed the plates off their trays, the boy noticed that the table was covered with what looked like a bed sheet. He felt it ... no, the fabric was thicker than sheets. He didn't see any paper napkins, so he wondered if maybe it was something special to wipe your hands and mouth on. As they ate, he watched. No, no one was doing that. So he wiped his mouth on his sleeve instead.

Slightly embarrassed, Karl pointed to the cloth napkin that was set up like a little tent in front of his plate. "Use that," he said kindly.

Hiding smiles, the others at the table pretended not to notice.

Out of courtesy toward the child, the Star People chatted, but in the boy's language. One looked at Little Monkey and asked, "Are you here on a visit?"

"No, sir, I'm here on official business."

They laughed pleasantly.

"No, he really is," Karl smiled. "We both are."

They continued their chatting. "Is the boy the first native child to come aboard a starship?" one Star Person asked.

"No, there was one other, a little girl ... a couple of years ago. She was brought up for extensive emergency surgery and stayed several days," another answered.

And so they talked on: "How long have you been away from home? Two years. How about you? Five years. Did you hear about the latest promotions?"

On and on they chatted. Then they talked of the fascinating things they had encountered on other planets: plants that crawled, rocks that sang, bugs that growled. The boy listened with wonder and awe. Everyone was so very nice, and as usual, the food was wonderful.

As he listened to the neatly uniformed people talk and laugh, he looked at the great viewscreen showing the glittering stars. At that moment he knew ... someday ... somehow ... he also would be a Star Man!

Chapter 5

Mountain Kids

On one of their flights in the small flyer, Karl noticed the boy's rapt attention to his movements of the controls. If there were such a rule as to *not* teach a much-too-young kid from another world how to pilot a flyer, Karl was sure he would be breaking it.

"Want to learn?"

Little Monkey looked at him in astonishment. "Do you mean fly the flyer?"

"Sure do!"

Little Monkey eagerly accepted. What fun it would be!

Karl turned the flyer away from the city and traveled until they arrived at a field between rolling hills. After they had landed, Karl slid the pilot seat back so that the boy could sit on the edge in front of him. He put his large hands over the boy's small ones and they operated the controls together. They took off, went high, low, forward, and even backward. The boy was ecstatic! When they landed, the boy moved over to his own seat, and Karl readjusted his.

"Thanks for letting me fly the flyer. It was lots of fun." Little Monkey smiled gratefully at Karl, and then asked, "Has a flyer ever crashed before?"

"I suppose so, but I've never heard of one. These little flyers are quite tough." Then Karl looked over to the boy and said, "If we ever were to crash, I would want you to put your feet up here." He patted the dash and the boy put his feet up. "This would help cushion you against a forward drop. It's not much, but it would be something. We don't have seatbelts like your surface cars do."

"Do you drive those cars too?"

"No, they are too small for us and not very comfortable. I would bump my head and have to drive like this ..." Karl cocked his head over to his shoulder and let his tongue hang out.

He looked so funny that the boy could hardly stop giggling.

* * *

It was a typical evening and they were finishing dinner in the kitchen, as usual. "Boy, go get me a couple more of those dessert cups, please," Gio asked.

Little Monkey jumped down off his chair, eager to please. Karl gave Gio a disapproving look.

"What?" said Gio. "The boy's legs are a lot younger than my old ones. After all, I've been on my feet all day, making you this feast fit for a king!"

"Boy, while you're up, get me one too, please!" another officer called out.

Karl gave him a disapproving look also. "The boy is not our slave, you know."

"Does anyone else want one?" Little Monkey called from the buffet table.

"Yes, get me one too," a third man called back, laughing.

Karl gave him a look too. "Now, what's your excuse? Are your legs broken?"

After a few moments had passed, Karl also called to the boy, "Get me another one, too!"

Then they all laughed. Karl knew the men were not interested in using the child. The atmosphere was more like that of a family, helping each other.

Little Monkey carefully balanced five dessert cups on a plate and brought them back to the table. Each man said, "Thanks, boy."

As he walked back to the buffet table to get himself one, he thought ... even though they all know my name is Little Monkey, they call me boy. But I don't care. He grinned. I don't care at all—they can call me anything they want. He licked the puff of cream off the top of his dessert. Just as long as they call me for dinner!

* * *

Karl was giving Little Monkey another lesson in piloting the flyer. They had gone to a rather remote area in the hills—to a large field next to a lake. The boy sat in front of Karl as before, and with his hand on the boy's, they went up and down, forward and back. It was tedious for Karl, but the boy really enjoyed it.

They landed the flyer, and the boy slipped over into his seat. They were about to leave, but a movement at the edge of the nearby woods caught Karl's eye. "Look over there," he whispered to the boy.

Little Monkey followed Karl's gaze and saw two children crouching in the tall grass. They probably had seen the flyer rising up and going down over the tree tops and were curious, and came to investigate.

"Do you want to go talk to them? So they won't be afraid?" Karl asked.

"Sure!" Little Monkey said as he hopped out of the flyer and immediately started off toward them.

"Hi!" he called.

The two children didn't answer, but they didn't run away either.

"Hi! Did you see me fly the Star People flyer? It was so much fun!"

He was near enough to see the two children plainly—a boy and a younger little girl.

"Do you want to come see it?" He pointed back behind him at the flyer. "You don't have to be scared of it."

Karl was walking toward them also, but keeping at a distance.

"Who is *that*!" The boy looked nervously at Karl as he approached.

"Oh, his name is Commander Karl. He's my friend! He let me fly the flyer!"

"Hi, kids," Karl said, stopping a short distance before reaching them. "You don't have to be afraid. We are all friends here."

The little girl looked up at the man towering over them. "Are you a giant?"

Before Karl could answer, Little Monkey giggled. "No, he's not. I thought the Star People were all giants too, but they aren't, and they are really nice."

"Are you two kids alone here in the woods?" Karl asked

"No, we live up here. My mom and dad and us."

"Mommy is really bad sick," the little girl said sadly.

"She's sick? How long has she been sick?" Karl questioned gently.

"Not long," said the boy, "but we are real worried. I even saw my dad cry."

Little Monkey, taking the initiative asked, "Does she have the plague? Did you all get the plague medicine?"

The kids looked confused, so Little Monkey raised his sleeve and showed them the little black circle. "Here is where I got mine." His voice was muffled into his sleeve. Then he twisted and

52

showed them the other little black circle on his other arm. "We get two of them."

"You got tattoos!" the boy exclaimed.

"I guess, but it's the medicine ... so you won't get the plague."

"Can I get tattoos?" the boy asked eagerly.

Karl and Little Monkey looked knowingly at each other, and Karl said, "Sure you can! My boy here can give them to you. To both of you."

The boy eagerly agreed, but the little girl asked, "Does it hurt?"

"No," Karl assured her. "It just feels a tiny bit warm when it is put on your arm, that's all. Doesn't hurt at all, I promise."

While the kids chatted, Karl went back to the flyer and soon returned with a pack of syringes. Karl quickly instructed Little Monkey on how to administer the medicine. "Put the tip on the arm, and push this button. Tell them not to move. Wait for the little green light to turn off. Then put the tip on the other arm, and push the second button. It only takes a second for each."

Karl turned to the kids, "Who wants to go first?"

The little girl quickly pointed to her brother and said, "Him!"

When Little Monkey was finished, the boy admired his new "tattoos." Since it obviously did not seem to hurt her brother, the little girl got her "tattoos" as well.

As the two children were comparing their arms, a man slowly emerged from the darkness of the woods. He had a rifle pointed straight at Karl! Karl, seeing the man, raised his arms and stepped in front of Little Monkey, placing himself between the weapon and the boy.

"Kids, get over here! Now!" The strange man ordered, keeping the rifle aimed at Karl. "You're one of those space aliens! Aren't you!"

"No, Dad ..." the kids tried to explain.

"Quiet!" he snapped at his children.

He took a step toward Karl. "What are you doing here! Why is that boy with you!"

"Please be calm, sir. We mean you no harm. My boy and I are here to help. I understand that your wife is sick. Is it the plague? If so, we can help. We have the medicine to cure it."

"That's a lie!" the man shouted. "There is no cure! You space aliens brought plague here so you can take over our world!"

"No, sir, that is not correct. The plague had decimated most of your planet's population before we even got here. We developed a cure, and have saved millions ... and we can save your wife too, if you'll let us."

"See, Dad? Susie and I got the medicine! It's a cool tattoo!"

"And it didn't even hurt!" Susie chimed in.

Little Monkey stepped out from behind Karl. "Sir, it's true. I have seen it with my own eyes. I saw sick people get well after getting the medicine. One of the kids I knew got sick and blood came out of his nose, so we took him to one of the places where they were giving the medicine tattoos, and in a few days, he was all better!"

The man's resolve began to melt. He was exhausted from worry and fear that his wife would die, and that they all would die. He lowered his rifle some. He was impressed that the big man from another world had stepped between them, protecting the boy who was obviously of *this* world. "Can you really save my wife?"

"Yes, absolutely ... as long as she ... hasn't been sick for too long a time."

"Alright then." The man lowered the rifle completely. "Come with me."

They started off for the family's home. It was a cozy cabin hidden among the tall trees. Karl had to duck through the doorway as they entered. The man ushered them to a bedroom where his wife lay. Karl was very much relieved to see that the sick woman was not beyond saving. He knelt next to her. She never even noticed as he administered the vaccine. Then the children's father rolled up his sleeves and received his.

It had gotten cooler, so the man started a fire in the cabin fireplace. Even though Karl was too big for the chair, they sat around the crackling fire and talked with the family for a while. Karl promised to return with some gasoline for the man's truck so he could get to the nearest town for supplies. Dusk was approaching, so Karl and Little Monkey left before it became too dark to see the path back to the flyer.

The next day, when they returned with gasoline as promised, the mother was already showing signs of recovery. The father and his children were very grateful to the alien Star Man and his boy.

* * *

"Want to go on a picnic?" Karl asked.

"What's that?" Little Monkey responded.

"Well, it's like we pack a lunch and go eat it in a nice place, like a field next to a lake."

"Why? Why not eat here where there are no flies?"

Karl chuckled, "Do you remember Senior Airman Alana? She brought me papers to sign? At my office?"

"Oh, yes, I remember. She also came when we were eating lunch one time."

"Correct. She is assigned to help find people who have not been vaccinated for the plague, and I thought that she might want to meet the people from the mountain, you know, the family with the sick mother."

Little Monkey nodded.

"She's going to pack us a lunch, to eat up there at the lake. Isn't that a nice idea?"

Little Monkey shrugged his shoulders. There would be flies. He hated flies.

"We'll also bring more syringes of vaccine to the mountain family in case they find people who haven't gotten the medicine, and also see if they need anything else."

*

So, they went on a picnic. After delivering the supplies to the mountain family, whose mother was now totally well, the mountain boy walked back with them to the lake. He taught Little Monkey how to skip flat little rocks across the water, while Senior Airman Alana and Commander Karl spread a large cloth on the ground. She then opened a big basket full of food. The lady was very nice, he had to admit, as she distributed sandwiches and fruit drinks.

There were flies, but the two Star People did not seem to notice. They ate and talked together, smiling constantly. Little Monkey and the mountain boy ate, then continued to skip rocks across the lake. After about an hour, the mountain boy went home. The lady and Karl were lying down on the cloth, propped up by their elbows, and still talking and smiling ... constantly smiling. Little Monkey wondered ... if someone smiles too much, would their faces freeze that way?

They needed to get back before the afternoon transports left for the orbiting ships, so they packed up and entered the flyer. Karl and Alana were still talking and smiling. They were so engrossed with each other, Little Monkey figured that even if he stood on his head in the back seat, they probably wouldn't even notice. He felt a little bit of jealousy ... he couldn't help it.

When the flyer landed at the landing field, the lady left for the transport that would take her back to her ship. Little Monkey and Karl then flew back to the hotel, saying little. The boy looked up at

Karl, and just rolled his eyes and shook his head. Karl was still smiling.

*

As the days passed, sometimes word would come in that there might be a group of homeless children wandering the streets in plague devastated areas. The protocol (established procedure) was to set out food, and if it were eaten, more was set out. Hidden cameras would confirm if the hungry ones were indeed children. If so, then Little Monkey would come and talk to them. He would try to convince them to go into fully monitored group homes and orphanages where they would be safe. Sometimes the kids agreed quickly, but some required more effort to convince them. Little Monkey insisted on working with each group until they agreed to be helped.

Commander Karl had other duties, so he did not accompany them on the "save the street children" missions, but the Star Lady Alana often did. She really was a very nice person, and Little Monkey grew to like her very much. Sometimes Karl would invite her to join them for dinner—to talk about the missions, he would say. But Little Monkey was no fool. It wasn't the missions; it was because Karl liked being with her ... maybe it was because she always smelled like flowers.

Chapter 6

Star Man's Son

As the boy sat quietly drawing, Karl noticed him constantly brushing his hair from his eyes. He obviously needed another haircut. An appointment was made for the next afternoon after school.

*

Little Monkey climbed into the weird chair.

"So, how short do you want it?" the barber asked as he tucked fabric around the boy's neck.

"I want my hair like ... his!" The boy lifted his pointing finger under the cloth and nodded his head toward Karl.

"OK then, no problem."

The barber trimmed the top of the boy's straight dark hair to about three inches, then tapered the sides and back gradually shorter and shorter, ending with a neat trim at the base of his neck and around his ears. Since the boy was too young to shave, he wouldn't have the perfect sideburns that Karl had, so the barber left some hair longer in front of and down to nearly the bottom of his ears, so the effect would be the same.

As he watched hair fall to the floor, Karl was touched by the boy's desire to be like him ... just like a boy who wants to be like his father.

Then, an idea began to form deep within him.

*

One night Karl and Little Monkey were relaxing on the couch together, watching a movie about a boy and his pet dog. The boy got lost, and the dog helped the worried father find his lost son. Just when the boy was about to fall off a cliff, the dog saved him. The dad was overjoyed as he hugged and kissed his son. He was so happy that he even kissed the dog.

As Little Monkey watched the touching reunion, he felt the familiar pang of loss—of something missing—a father. He glanced sideways at Karl and then back to the movie, and sure that Star Man Karl would not hear, he barely whispered, "I wish you were my dad."

But Karl *did* hear. He gently turned the boy's face to him. "What did you say?"

Dreading the response to such an obviously ridiculous idea, he lowered his eyes and said "I ... I said that I wish that you were my dad."

"Do you mean that?"

He nodded, looking up into the big man's questioning face.

Karl smiled. "I didn't want to mention it until I knew for sure, but I have been looking into the possibility of adopting you. If my request is approved, I would become your legal parent—your dad, and you would be my son."

"For real?"

"Yes," Karl smiled, "for real. But, I want you to understand something." Karl's smile faded into seriousness. "My duty tour here will be up in about a year, and then I will go home to my world ... and as my child, you would come with me. Do you understand what that means? You would be leaving your world, possible forever."

"I don't care! I just want to be with you!" The boy could hardly contain his joy. Why, Star Man Karl could adopt any kid he wanted—but he picked me! Then he quickly thought, how silly! Of course he picked me, he knows me the best.

"When will you know if I can be your son?" he asked eagerly.

"It shouldn't be much longer." Karl laughed and then said, "Do you think that you would like a different name other than 'Little Monkey'? After all, you are a *boy*, not a monkey!"

"Yes," the boy paused, then he hopped off the couch, stood up straight and saluted perfectly. "Yes, sir! I would like my name to be Star Man Commander Karl's Son!"

"That's quite a mouthful." Karl smiled broadly. "Let's see ... how about ... Karlson?"

"I like that!" he exclaimed happily as he threw his arms around Karl's neck and hugged him tightly. "I'm the luckiest kid in the world!"

Karl smiled, returning the boy's hug. Now it was his turn to feel like the luckiest in the world.

*

Before the adoption could be processed and approved, every effort needed to be made to find information on Little Monkey's parents or extended family. So, they met with two ladies at the orphanage. The women had searched through their records, but found nothing on the child "Little Monkey." Since the orphanage had been established the records had been poorly kept, so they were incomplete and totally inadequate. They had no choice but to interview the boy, but he had no memories that he could recall prior to being at the orphanage.

"What do you remember? Do you remember being called any name other than 'Little Monkey'?"

"I think they called me 'kid.' That's all I remember ... and I want my name to be Karlson. Little Monkey is a little kid's name."

The ladies smiled and agreed. "Was it summer or winter when you ran away from the orphanage?"

The boy thought for a while. "When I ran away, it was cold. I remember because I didn't have any shoes on. I didn't know where to go. I saw some kids and I followed them into a big place that had lots of food. I recognized Jake and another boy from the orphanage—they ran away from it before I did. The gang leader let me stay with them, and we ate food from cans, and we hid in a dark room in the back of that place. There was a nice lady who came there all the time, and she took us all to her house. It was warm there and she made us beds on the floor. It was real nice. Then she got sick ... she had blood coming out of her eyes ... and then she was dead. Her room got terribly stinky—it was so bad that I threw up. We all left and went back to the food place, but all the food was gone."

He paused, remembering, "Then we made a plan. We decided for each of us to follow a grown-up who was getting on a bus, so the bus driver would think we were with them and let us get on too. We didn't know where it was going, but we hoped it would be a place that was warm and had food."

He paused again. "I remember summer was real hot, and I remember that our gang leader and another boy were grabbed by some mean men, and we never saw them again. That's when Jake became our leader.

"It got cold again, and we lived in lots of different houses where people were dead ... they were mostly all dried up, so they didn't stink so much. We made fires in the fireplaces, but people would come and we had to run and hide, and then look for another house.

61

"Then it was hot again. We kept moving from house to house, eating the food that was in cans. When there were no more houses with food, we had to walk a long way to find more."

The boy was silent for a moment, remembering. "Then it got cold again. We found the tipped over bus, and lived there. It wasn't dark inside because of the windows that were on top now—because it was tipped over. It even had a back door that we could lock from the inside ... it was pretty safe there. We made a fire every night in a big metal thing that Jake dragged home. He opened a window on the top for the smoke to get out. It was pretty good there."

The two ladies and Karl listened intently.

"When we could, we stole food from the Star People; they didn't lock anything so it was pretty easy ... sorry. But it was still hard to find enough food. We got good at catching rats. We cooked them, but they didn't taste very good ... but it was better than nothing."

The listening ladies dabbed tears from their eyes, and Karl blinked quickly trying to remove the moisture forming in his.

"Then it was summer again, and I met the Star People when they caught me getting food for the gang, and now it's cold again."

"I counted three years to present," one of the ladies said. "If he came to you this past summer, Commander Karl, then he and the others had been surviving on the streets for 2½ years. Amazing."

The lady wrote some information on her papers. "We need to enter a birth date for Little ... for Karlson on the forms," she said as she looked at the boy, studying him. "He looks to be between ten and eleven years old now, so a good estimate would be that he is approximately 10½."

"What do you suggest?" the other lady asked Karl.

But before he could answer, the boy asked Karl, "What was the day when you first caught me?"

Karl remembered clearly. "It was the 15th of July," he replied.

"That should be my new birth date! Is that OK?" he asked eagerly.

The lady glanced at Karl, and seeing his approval, wrote July 15th on her papers.

"That should be my birth date," Karlson smiled, "because that's when my new life started."

Chapter 7

BOMB!

Their first place did not have a balcony, but this larger place did. Since Commander Karl was the Commanding Officer of Sector Seven, he could have taken any one of the fancy apartments on the upper levels of the hotel when he had first arrived, but he didn't. It just didn't matter to him. But when the boy started staying with him, he then decided to move to a suite with two bedrooms. It was really nice, because you could see across the whole city from up there.

One night Karlson sat on the cold balcony floor with his feet and legs dangling out between the rails. Even though it was very quiet, sometimes he would wake up during the night and come out. He enjoyed the serene view. The stars were bright, and sometimes the moon looked close enough to reach out and touch. But this night, the floor was a bit too cold, so he got up and perched himself on top of the railing. Looking down at the swimming pool far below him, he wondered if anyone had jumped into it from this high up—not that *he* would! That would be crazy!

Leaning back against the wall that the balcony rail was attached to, he thought about how happy he was that his adoption had been approved. He was now officially Karl's son. He finally had a dad! Suddenly, he heard a noise from behind him inside the partially open balcony doors. He held his breath and nervously waited. Did Dad wake up?

It was nothing. He was glad that his dad had not awakened. He didn't want to be caught up on the balcony railing. It wasn't that he was being disobedient, he just knew that his dad wouldn't understand. He looked down. After all, being a "Little Monkey," he had climbed higher than this before.

Then his keen eyes detected movement below. Two shadows were quietly moving at the base of the hotel. Even though they were keeping their voices low, the sounds echoed up to his perch, and he could hear them plainly.

"Hurry up!"

"Don't rush me! It's almost ready."

He knew those voices! It was the two bad boss men from the orphanage that had been taken away—but they were supposed to be in jail!

"There, I set it for 10 minutes. That will give us plenty of time to get far away before it blows."

"Yeah, those self-righteous star jerks are going to get theirs!"

Blows?? What did that mean? Then Karlson knew. Bomb! He knew what bombs were. One of the other gangs made one and tried to blow the back door off a place where food was kept. It didn't work out so well for them!

Karlson jumped down and raced to his dad's room. "Dad! Wake up! I think those bad men put a bomb out back!"

"Wha...?"

"A bomb! Out back! What do we do?"

Karl was now wide awake. "Did you have a dream?"

"No, Dad, this is real!" Karlson insisted as he pulled on Karl's arm. "I heard them say it would blow in ten minutes!"

Realizing the boy did not seem to have nightmares, and the fact that he was so wide awake made Karl jump into action. Barefooted and only in their underwear, they both ran out the door and into the elevator—it would be quicker than the steps. Still, the elevator felt like it took *forever* for the doors to ding and slide open.

They burst out, ran across the lobby, and quickly unlocked one of the back doors. Karl shouted, "Where?"

"There!" the boy pointed. "Over near the big windows!"

They ran over and to Karl's horror, there it was. He fell to his knees to see it clearly. It had 5 minutes left on the timer. He didn't know its composition, and there was no time to even try to disarm it.

"Stay here!" he shouted to the boy as he picked up the evil thing. "Stay here! I mean it!"

Then Karl ran. He ran as fast as he could toward a big field nearby, away from any occupied buildings. The locals had called it a football field. His breathing was fast and heavy as his feet pounded toward the field. Almost there! He glanced at the timer. Two minutes to go! He had reached the field. Here! He put it down in the middle of the football field. One and a half minutes! He spun around and began running back. He counted down the time as he ran, ignoring the pain in his legs and bare feet. At five seconds, he dove to the ground and put his hands over the back of his head and neck.

BOOM!

The ground shook and the sky lit up. Fragments of cold dirt and grass splattered down on Karl's back. He kept down until he could feel nothing more falling on him. Then he got up and looked behind him. The football field was no more. Instead, it had become a huge smoking pit.

Karl shook his body trying to rid himself of the debris, and then he started back at a gentle jog—which instantly turned into a painful walk. His feet really hurt. He could see the hotel in the distance. Lights were coming on in many room windows. As he approached, he could see several men standing outside. Then he saw Karlson calling and running toward him.

"Dad!" Karlson ran into him, almost knocking him off his sore feet. "Are you OK?"

"Yes, son, I'm OK."

The boy flipped the blanket (someone had put on him) up to his dad. Karl unfolded it and wrapped it around his shivering shoulders and also around the boy. Karlson could see that his dad was limping, so he hugged him tighter and tried to help him walk.

Several men jogged toward them. "You alright, Commander?" Everyone was talking all at once. "What happened?"

More and more people came out. "Did something blow up?"

With the aid of several men, Karl sat down in one of the chairs on the hotel patio. He looked at his sore feet—they were bleeding. One of the men brought him a robe. "We're taking you to the clinic. I'll call old Doc so he can meet you there."

"I'm fine."

"No, we're taking you."

"Who outranks who here?" Karl laughed as they got him up. He hobbled with them to a flyer that had just landed on the grass. Karlson was right behind them.

*

After getting patched up and taking a much needed shower, Karl joined his son and they went down to breakfast. The police were there waiting for them. They both told their stories (but Karlson left out the part where he had been sitting precariously up on the balcony rail). Nearly everyone from the hotel was there and listened patiently. Before they left, the police officers assured the Star Men that the two perpetrators would soon be found, and they would let Karl know how those two got out of jail.

Karlson was glad to see the police leave—he was starving! They went to the kitchen where Gio was waiting, keeping the food warm. After they had gone through the buffet and sat eating, all conversation was of the bomb. Everyone congratulated and thanked Karl for risking his life to carry it to a safe distance.

But Karlson was the big hero.

"That bomb was powerful. It would have taken the entire building down, and we all would most likely have been killed," one officer said.

Then another interrupted, "Boy, do you realize what you did? You saved all our lives!"

As he looked from one smiling grateful face to another, and with clarity of thought beyond his years, the boy said softly, "You saved mine first."

Chapter 8

Going Down!

They were on their way back from visiting Sector Eight, where one of Karl's friends was the commanding officer. It was a nice spring day—bright and sunny, but a bit hot. The flyer passed between very high hills, or small mountains—depending on how you look at it. As they traveled, they flew over a huge dirt pit. Karl explained that it was the site of an explosion of a power plant that had become unmanned during the plague, and therefore went out of control.

Suddenly the flyer fell in a sickening drop. Then it jerked up and forward as the engine picked up again. Karl instinctively raised his arm in front of the boy to keep him from being thrown forward as the flyer lost speed. Not a second later, the flyer engine cut out again and they dropped. Karl shouted a word that the boy did not understand, then exclaimed anxiously, "Hang on! We're going down!"

Karlson was frightened. His hands gripped the sides of his seat tightly.

"Put your feet up!"

He did as he remembered his dad showing him.

Karl struggled with the controls, trying to veer the craft toward the flat ground at the edge of the huge crater as the engine cut in and out. The ground was coming up fast! Karl again put his arm out to protect Karlson from being thrown forward. Luckily, the engine engaged just before they were about to crash. Karl managed a less-than-perfect landing a few yards away from the pit edge. He cut the power and the flyer rolled forward several feet and stopped.

"You OK?" He turned to the boy.

With his brown eyes big as saucers, Karlson nodded and asked, "What happened?"

"Don't know. This is rare, in fact, it almost never happens." He pressed the communication button on the radio, but instead of the familiar hum, they heard static. "It must be interference from the mountains," Karl murmured, mostly to himself.

"Let's see if we can fix this thing." He turned in his seat and removed a heavy bag of tools from a compartment in the floor between the seats. They both got out and he opened a hatch door at the rear of the flyer. Karl was engrossed with finding the engine problem until he noticed the boy peering over the edge of the pit.

"No!" he yelled. "Get away from the edge!"

The startled boy jumped back.

Then Karl said more gently, "Come, help me fix this."

Karlson did as he was told, and together they peered into the complicated engine.

"Found it!" Karl exclaimed. "The connector for a harness of wiring has come loose in its socket. See?" He held it forward for Karlson to see. "The lock over it popped off ... somehow."

He fiddled a bit more inside the engine. "That about does it!" Karl said as he closed the engine hatch. Stepping away from the flyer and wiping the sweat from his face onto his shirt, he said,

"Let's get some cold drinks from the cooler. How does that sound?"

"Sounds great," Karlson grinned.

Suddenly, the ground shifted and started to fall into the huge pit. Landslide! As the ground disintegrated under them, they madly clawed at the crumbling rocks and dirt, scrambling to regain footing. Even with his great strength, Karl couldn't keep from sliding. He knew he was going down, so he quickly grabbed Karlson with both hands, and with all his might, he threw the boy up to the solid ground next to the flyer, which forced himself to further slip helplessly down into the ravine.

The boy did not notice his scraped hands as he turned and crawled back to the edge of the landslide. He could not see anything below through the thick dust. He screamed for his dad. There was no answer. In panic, he called and called. Then, as the dust settled, he could see Karl below, half covered in dirt and rocks.

He wasn't moving.

The greatest fear the boy had ever felt overcame him. He was more frightened than when that big black spider crawled across his face. He was more frightened than when he tried to catch a rat that almost bit him. He was even more frightened than when that bad boss man grabbed him at the orphanage.

Karlson anxiously thought to himself: Get a grip! What can I do? I have to go to Dad. But how can I do that? Then he remembered. Check the flyer! There should be an emergency pack behind the back seats!

He quickly crawled backward away from the ravine edge and opened the door to the flyer. Yes! There it was. He dragged out the large heavy pack and opened it. A rope! The trees were too far away. What could he tie the rope to? Then he decided to tie it to the flyer. He tied a good strong knot, then spread the rope out and threw it over the side of the cliff.

Remembering how he and the gang once carried jars and jars of baby food that they had found, he pulled the looseness of the bottom of his shirt forward and tied it into a knot so that it was tight against his body. He then dropped a small first-aid medical kit plus two water bottles down into the "pocket" that he had made inside his shirt.

Ignoring the pain in his palms, he got a good tight grip on the rope. True to his former name, with relative ease he hand-over-hand held onto the rope as he scrambled and slid down the wall of loose dirt to the bottom of the pit. He made it! Fearing the worst, he ran over to Karl.

"Dad! Dad!" he called as he threw the rocks off Karl's body.

Karl moaned. He was alive!

Karl opened his eyes to see the anxious tear-streaked little face above him. "Son, are you OK?" he whispered. "What ... what happened?"

"The ground fell. You fell! Can you get up? I have a rope."

Karl attempted to move and yelped in pain. His leg was broken.

*

It was still hot, but the creeping shadow from the late afternoon sun was almost upon them. Karlson gave his father a drink of water, and tried to wipe the dirt from his face. Then he tossed the remaining small rocks off Karl, looking for wounds. With things from the first-aid kit, he cleaned the bleeding scrapes that he could see and put bandages on them.

But he didn't know what to do about the broken bone, as he watched his father grimace with pain. He was afraid to even touch the leg—that obviously lay at an unnatural angle. Then Karl was silent. Karlson frantically touched his dad's face, calling to him.

Karl was unconscious, but breathing steadily.

Karlson knew what he must do—he had to get help. He put the second bottle of water in his dad's motionless hand, and then, as quickly as he could, climbed back up the rope to the flyer.

Could he do this? Could he pilot the flyer up out of the valley, high enough to call for help? He had never flown alone before! What if he made a mistake and crashed? No one would come to help Dad! What other choice did he have? He couldn't walk out of this place. Dad might die if they just waited for someone to eventually come looking for them. He had to do this! There was no other choice! Then, with a sudden rush of confidence he said out loud, "I am a Star Man's Son! I *can* do this!"

He untied the rope from the flyer and then climbed into the pilot's seat, sitting on the front edge. He carefully went over each step in his mind before attempting anything. Satisfied, he pushed the engine-on button. He gratefully felt the very faint vibration, and the lights on the instrument panel came on.

He clinched his jaw and raised the lift lever gently. The flyer went up! About ten feet off the ground, he set the lift to neutral, and then gently pushed the drive control yoke forward. The craft slowly moved away from the nearby grove of trees. He pulled the yoke back to neutral, then again carefully raised the lift lever. His dad skillfully always operated both the lift and the forward at the same time, but he wasn't even going to try that.

Up he went until he had cleared the highest mountain top. He set the lift back to neutral. As the craft hovered, he pushed the radio control button and called as he had remembered his dad doing so many times.

"This is Karlson calling Sector Seven."

The answer came back immediately. "This is Sector Seven. Karlson, where is the Commander?"

"He's hurt bad! He needs help! Can you come now?"

"Yes, hold on. Yes, we have your location. You ... are not on the ground?"

"No, sir, I'm in the flyer. Dad fell down over the cliff. He has a broken leg!"

"You are alone ... in the flyer ... in the air?"

"Yes, sir"

"Alright. Stay right there. Don't touch any of the controls. The Medical Team will be there in about 15 minutes. Don't attempt to land, OK?"

"OK, but please hurry."

"The Med Team will be there before you know it. Now, tell me what happened."

The man at Sector Seven kept Karlson talking until the large Medical flyer plus two other flyers arrived.

"Karlson," the man on the radio said, "we are concerned as to what to do with you. We can't leave you in the flyer. Do you know how to land it?" the voice asked hopefully.

"I think so. I have done it before, but with my dad."

Then another voice cut in. "I can see the boy. There is a clearing up ahead. Karlson, do you see it?"

"Yes, sir."

"I'm right next to you."

Karlson looked over and saw another flyer hovering next to his.

"I am going to stay right with you and we are going to land together, OK?"

"Yes, sir." Karlson answered, with more confidence than he felt.

As the other pilot instructed, he gently pushed the drive yoke forward and turned it slowly, remembering his father's words—small moves only. They stopped high above a clearing that was a safe distance from the pit. Then they descended together ever so slowly. The pilot next to him called out the distance to the ground, "five feet … four … three … two … one … down! Now cut your engine!"

Karlson gratefully felt the craft touch the ground and he quickly turned the engine off.

"Great landing, kid! You did a better job than I did when I was a Cadet at the Academy!"

Karlson scarcely heard him as he opened the door and hopped out to the ground, and then ran to the other waiting flyer. They lifted off, and in seconds arrived at the bottom of the ravine. Before the pilot had cut the engine, Karlson was out the door and running toward his father. The Med Team had already gotten Karl onto an antigravity stretcher, which was moving effortlessly toward the open bay doors of the large medical flyer. Karl was still unconscious, but his face was relaxed.

"Don't worry, kid," one of the Medical Technicians assured him. "He'll be just fine."

Karlson held onto the side of the stretcher and walked alongside it. There was no way they were going to keep him from riding with his dad to the hospital.

*

Karl awoke in a hospital bed. He saw Karlson curled up in a chair, sound asleep. "He won't leave," whispered a voice next to him.

He turned his head to the nurse standing beside his bed. "How long have I been here?" Karl asked hoarsely.

"Just since yesterday," she said gently. "You broke your leg, but it was a clean break. You'll be up and around before you know it."

Karlson, aroused by the voices, rubbed his eyes and quickly came to his father's bedside.

"Hey, little man, are you OK?"

"Of course, Dad. I didn't fall—you did!"

Karl reached out and touched the boy's hair, "Yes, I sure did, didn't I? Tell me all about it. I don't remember much."

Karlson told him the events of that awful day. As he told the story, Karl looked at his boy. He was so proud of his son. "You're quite a kid! But I guess our secret is out ...."

"Huh? What secret?" Karlson asked, puzzled.

"The secret of me teaching you how to pilot the flyer!"

"Oh, yeah," Karlson grinned broadly, "I guess it is!"

*

When Karl was released from the hospital, he was issued crutches plus a motorized wheelchair. Karlson would stand on the back of the chair and together they whizzed down the carpeted hotel hallway, into the elevator, and down to meals. It was almost as much fun as when he rode that red and black Super Rider.

A couple of days after Karl had gotten home, Cook Gio brought a present—a video game! Karlson knew what it was, but had never played one. He could hardly wait as Gio hooked it up to the video screen.

It was so great! After school, they would play for hours. Sometimes they would eat something called "pizza" as they played. Karlson was glad that his dad did not treat him like a little kid and just let him win ... well, maybe in the beginning he might have, but now they both played their best. His dad sometimes said: "For a boy to become a man, he should be expected to act like a man, and not be babied," then he would always add "within reason, of course." Sitting next to his dad—both with their feet up—playing "Jet Race," he smiled to himself: I am the luckiest kid in the world. In fact, I am the luckiest kid in all the worlds!

Chapter 9

I Don't Lie

Karlson was growing. With proper nutrition, his skinny body filled out and he was getting taller. So, he and his dad took another trip to the warehouse. As Karl selected some new clothes for the boy, Karlson eagerly found the red and black Super Rider. He plopped down into the reclining seat and began to pedal, but was surprised that his knees almost hit the handlebars! He rode over to his father.

Noticing how the boy was too big for the child-sized toy, he exclaimed, "You really *have* grown!"

When they left the warehouse and got back into the flyer, Karl glanced back at the storage area in the rear, and then said mysteriously, "I have an idea."

"What is it?"

"Are you game for a little trip to one of the empty zones?"

"Sure!" Karlson said excitedly. The empty zones were places where no one lived anymore. The plague bodies had been removed, but the population needed to grow more before the empty towns and cities would be needed.

The trip took about half an hour, and when they got there, Karl piloted their craft slowly down the streets of the deserted town, carefully avoiding the dead power lines above, until he found the store that he was looking for. He landed the flyer in a partially empty parking lot nearby. There was debris everywhere. The cool wind blew scraps of paper and leaves across their path as they walked the eerily silent street. A sudden gust blew something white toward them. It crookedly rolled about until it lay still. Dark hollow eyes stared up at them.

It was a skull! A human skull! Karlson bent down to get a stick ... he wanted to go get a good look at it and maybe open its partially toothless jaw, but Karl pulled him back.

"No, son. That was once a person. We must show respect," he said softly. "Before we leave, we'll put a beacon near it and have someone come and try to find the rest of him, and take care of him properly." He put his hand gently on the boy's shoulder. "Let's go."

They left the skull and entered the broken-out window of the store Karl had been looking for. In the dim light Karlson could see ... bicycles! Hundreds of bicycles! It was dark in there since the power was off in the entire town, but Karl had brought a powerful flashlight.

"Let's find you a bike!" he said to the ecstatic boy.

*

It was cool outside, and nearly everyday Karlson would ride his bright blue bike. His dad had shown him how. First Dad had him stand on a narrow board and keep his balance. Then he had him shut his eyes and try to keep his balance. After that, he showed him how to sit on the bike and push himself along with his feet, and then lift them a little and keep going ... without falling! When Karlson felt ready, he put his feet on the pedals and off he went ... he only crashed twice.

It was such fun! He was only allowed to ride during the day, and only around the hotel's general area. At night he brought the bike in and parked it in the storage room off the kitchen. Then one day it started to rain ... and it rained and rained. He wanted to ride!

On one of those rainy nights he woke up and couldn't go back to sleep. He didn't go out on the balcony as it was far too wet. Instead, he crept out of the apartment and went down the elevator. No one was awake, and wouldn't be for several hours. He had never been told *not* to ride inside, but he knew he probably shouldn't. But maybe he could ... maybe this once ... just ride a little ... just a little.

So, he brought the bike out of the storage room, and rode around the large kitchen. He needed more space so he rode through the sprawling lobby, down the halls, and back again into the large kitchen. Around and around he rode—faster and faster! He became an expert at dodging furniture in his path. Back in the kitchen, he must have hit a slippery spot because he suddenly lost his balance and the bike slid ... right into a rack of pans, and that rack rolled and bumped into a shelf—a shelf full of dishes ... which all crashed to the floor and sprayed out into a million pieces.

Karlson got up, unhurt, and rolled his bike back into the storage room. What should he do? Should he clean up the mess? But how? Pieces of dishes were everywhere! If he cleaned it up somehow ... but then Cook Gio would see that the dishes were gone. What to do? Finally, he decided to do nothing but go back upstairs and go back to bed. Maybe Gio would think the dishes fell by themselves.

*

The next morning at breakfast, Karlson watched unhappily as everyone blamed and teased Cook Gio about the mess. They joked him, saying things like "he was getting too old," or "he can't see straight enough to stack dishes," and stuff like that. They weren't being mean, but it wasn't fair to Gio ... should I tell them?

In the streets, you always lied, especially if you were caught doing something. But then he thought: Star Men do not lie. I am a Star Man's son, so I don't lie.

Karl sat watching and said nothing. He knew who did it, for he could plainly see a black bicycle tire skid-mark on the floor. He waited, hoping ... then Karlson stood up.

"I ... I did it. I knocked over the dishes."

Everyone looked at him. "I was riding my bike ..."

"Inside?" Karl interrupted, looking at him sternly. "You should have known better."

"Yes," Karlson hung his head. "I'm sorry."

"No bike for a week," Karl said flatly.

"Oh, it's not so bad ..." Gio began.

Karl shot him a look—stay out of it. Gio said no more.

*

On the ride to school Karlson said little. He didn't care about a week without the bike. He had let his dad down. Karl broke the silence and said to the miserable boy, "I'm proud of you, son."

Karlson was startled. Did he hear correctly? He looked up into his dad's serious face.

"You told the truth. You could have remained silent, but you stood up and told the truth. You acted like a man." He paused and then said with a little smile, "But still no bike for a week!"

Karlson didn't care about the loss of the bike. He was so happy. His dad didn't hate him!

* * *

It was a usual day, July 15, except that just about everyone came for dinner at the same time. Cook Gio had even added an extra table with chairs. Karlson was sitting on his specially raised chair with his feet swinging back and forth, eating another bread stick that was thickly smeared with butter, when suddenly the lights went out.

Karlson looked around the table, but no one seemed to care. Then Gio appeared with a cake that was on fire! Everyone called out "Happy Birthday!" and then started clapping. Karlson was confused as he realized that they were all smiling and looking at him!

"Today is your new birthday!" Karl said in his ear. "This is a birthday party!"

Karlson had never heard of such a thing. Gio put the flaming cake in front of him. He saw that the cake wasn't *really* burning; it was eleven little candles stuck in the cake that were on fire.

"Blow them out!" came the calls. "Blow out the candles!"

Karlson looked at his dad. Karl made a blowing motion, so Karlson took a deep breath and blew the candles out—all at one time!

Everyone clapped more. Then Gio rolled out a cart with packages on it. They were all wrapped with colored paper. "Go on," Gio said. "Unwrap one! They're all for you!"

Still confused, Karlson picked up one package and began to carefully open the seams where the paper was taped. "No, just rip it off!" voices called out from around the table.

So, he did.

The first gift was a crewman's hat with the starship name *Seeker* on it, written in the Star People's writing. "That's from me!" one of the officers said.

"This is great! I saw people on the ship wearing these!" he exclaimed as he put it on his head. "Thank you, sir!"

He ripped the paper off the next gift—it was a bright light for attaching to a bicycle. "That's from me," said Gio. "So if you ever get caught out when it gets dark ..." he paused and then said wryly, "or if you happen to be riding near my dishes again ...."

Everyone laughed, because they all knew the story. "That's not going to happen again, I promise, but thank you for the light! It will look great on my bike!"

The next gift was a black leather jacket covered with bright metal pieces. "That's from me!" another officer called from the end of the table. "It's a biker jacket."

"Wow!" It was the fanciest jacket he had ever seen! He started to put it on, but Karl said to wait, as it was too warm in the kitchen. "Thank you, sir!" he waved to the officer down at the end of the table.

Karlson kept opening his gifts. It was so much fun! He got a lot of great stuff, including a pair of really cool aviator style sunglasses, a game of checkers that Gio promised to teach him how to play, a dart board with sharp darts that his dad said *he* would teach him to play, and several new video games. From his dad he got a huge art set, complete with all kinds of different colored pencils, pens, and chalks plus shapes to trace designs with, stencils, colored paper, and about a zillion other things. It was great! He liked to draw!

Gio pulled the candles off the cake, licking the frosting off each, and then he cut and served the cake. It was the best cake Cook Gio had ever made. When it was all over, Karlson again thanked everyone for everything.

A birthday party! The happy boy thought to himself. Whoever came up with *that* idea was a genius!

It was a great day.

Chapter 10

Back to the Hotdog

Karlson was eager to practice piloting the flyer with his dad, and pestered him frequently. Karl wanted to teach his son, but "above board," with no secrets. He wanted official permission from the High Commander.

Karl could have simply called the starship orbiting above and asked for permission, but he thought the boy would enjoy another visit. Karlson eagerly agreed, so the next afternoon they boarded a transport. Karlson wore his new *Seeker* hat.

This transport was exactly the same as the first one except that the seats were a deep burgundy red instead of a deep blue. When all passengers were aboard, they took off. Karlson watched the land below shrink until the viewport blacked out for the "roll." While waiting for it to become clear again, he remembered his private joke that the transport looked like a huge egg going to the spaceship that looked like a hotdog wrapped in a giant fat bun.

He didn't realize he was smiling until Karl asked, "What's so funny?"

"Oh, it's nothing. I just think this ship looks like a big egg and the spaceship looks like a big hotdog!" he grinned. Then the viewport became clear. "See?"

Karl looked out of the viewport at the starship in the distance and chuckled, "I never thought of that before, but you're right. It does look like a skinny hotdog wrapped in a rotating bun."

"Rotating?"

"Yes, it is rotating. The main part of the starship hull revolves—slowly turns—around the central unmoving shaft thus producing a centrifugal force, which provides us a type of gravity. Look out there. See the red spot on the side of the hull? Now watch. It's moving ... see? The main hull of the ship, 'the bun,' is slowly rotating around the 'hotdog,' as you call it, which is the zero-gravity area. Do you see the round ends of the 'hotdog' that stick out of the 'bun'? Those are the arrays ... where the ships sensors are, front and back."

"Arrays? Is the front array the control room—where you fly the ship from?"

"No, the arrays are areas just for instruments, such as cameras and sensors. The control room is in the 'bun' part. It doesn't have to be in the front like it is in a flyer or a transport, where we need to actually *see* where we are going. In the control room, everything is electronic ... so we see what the cameras and other equipment pick up from the arrays. Actually, it would be very uncomfortable for the control room to be in the very front in the center, because that is a zero-gravity zone. Do you remember what I told you about gravity? How it's what makes everything have weight and keeps us down instead of just floating about?"

"I remember, but I thought you were just kidding me."

"No, not kidding. That's why the hotdog 'bun' is rotating around the hub—the skinny hotdog. The hull (the outer skin of the ship) is actually a floor for the interior, because the rotation of the hull causes everything inside to be ... sort of thrown outward, which gives us a feeling of gravity inside."

Karlson thought for a moment. "Like if I have a string and tie a rock on the end, and then twirl it around and around and then let go ... it flies away?"

"Yes, that 'away' part, is called centrifugal force, and is like 'extra gravity' that you made for the rock by spinning it."

"And," the boy eagerly said, "it's like on the playground. There is this thing that spins around. If you stand in the center, you just turn in circles, but if you are on the edge, you have to hold on tight or get spun off! And the faster it turns, the harder it is to hold on!"

"Exactly, that's centrifugal force."

"I think I get it!"

"I knew you would. You are a very smart young man. Gravity is ... tricky," Karl continued. "Natural gravity, like what we have on the planet surface, *pulls* us to the ground. But a manufactured gravity, by centrifugal force, *pushes* us outward, or down."

Karlson thought a moment and then asked. "Does that mean that the zero-gravity area is where everything would just float around?"

"Exactly," Karl replied. "We call it the 'Dead Zone.'"

"That's so cool! Can we go there sometime?"

His father laughed, "We'll see."

*

"Thank you for seeing us, sir," Karl said as he saluted. He tried not to smile when his son executed a perfect salute a split second after.

"At ease. So, Commander, you want to teach this young man here to pilot?"

"Yes, sir."

The High Commander glanced down at the file on his desk. "I see here that the boy *already* knows how to pilot a Class 1 flyer ... I wonder how *that* happened ..."

"Sir, I ..." Karl began to explain.

"Never mind, I know how it happened. I have the report." The High Commander smiled as he leaned back into his chair. "My dad taught me, and I taught my kids how to pilot before they were of proper age too ... I think we all do it."

He looked at Karlson. "So, do you think you're ready for the responsibility of learning to operate a flyer?"

Karlson gulped, "Yes, sir. I ..."

The High Commander interrupted, "I'll bet you would like to go really fast in one, right?"

Karlson stammered, "Uh, yes sir, I think it would be fun to go fast—I like to go fast on my bike."

"So you think that a flyer is like a bike—to have fun with?"

"Oh, no, sir. My bike is a toy because it's for kids. Dad says the flyer is not a toy."

"Your dad is right, it's NOT a toy. I hope you always remember that."

"Yes, sir." The boy said solemnly, "I promise."

"Alright Commander, you have permission to teach Karlson, but he must be supervised at all times—no solos—until he is of age and has passed the test."

"Thank you, sir," Karl said.

Then Karlson also quickly said, "Thank you, sir."

As the High commander handed Karl the signed form, he asked Karlson, "How old are you, son?"

"I'm eleven, I think, sir."

"We haven't been able to find any records," Karl interrupted, "so the orphanage had to estimate."

"Eleven, huh? Junior Cadets can enter the Academy at twelve. Now that he is your son—and I assume he will be accompanying you when you leave here—have you considered enrolling him?"

Both Karl and Karlson's eyes were wide with surprise.

"We haven't even thought about it, sir, but I would be very proud if he would like to join."

"What do you think of that, young man?" the High Commander asked the boy.

"Sir," fearing this Academy might be some sort of orphanage, he stammered, "Wha... What is the Academy?"

"It's a school, son, a very prestigious school. Boys and girls go there and when they graduate, they have many opportunities. They can even be Space Explorers, just like your dad."

"Like Dad? I want to be like Dad!"

"Sir, thank you for the suggestion," Karl said. "We will talk about it. My duty tour here won't be up for several more months, and then we'll see."

"You might want to get an application in earlier than that, Commander. Available slots for the Explorer Program fill fast."

"Yes, sir, thank you for the advice."

"Dismissed!" The High Commander said abruptly.

In unison, both Karl and Karlson saluted.

The High Commander leaned back into his big chair, smiling broadly. "Son, you already have the best salute I have ever seen from *any* Cadet!"

"Thank you, sir!" Karlson grinned, and then they left.

*

Karlson eagerly waited for the day he and his dad had planned for his first *official* flying lesson. To practice landings, they flew to a shallow lake surrounded by a grassy field. Karl switched places with his son and adjusted the pilot seat all the way forward, plus added a couple of seat cushions tucked behind him. If there were an accident, slamming down into the lake would be far less dangerous than the ground. Besides, the flyer could float if it remained upright.

So, by visual reference to his surroundings, Karlson got the feel of where the wheels on the skids underneath were in relation to the surface. At his first try, the water splashed up all around them. His second try was better. Up and down they went, until he mastered his "landing" of just barely touching the water surface.

When Karl thought he was ready, they moved off the lake and hovered above the field around the lake. Karlson was not nervous ... well, maybe just a tiny bit ... as he descended ever so slowly. He felt the wheels on the skids gently touch the ground. Both he and his dad were satisfied. They practiced a few more times before it was time to leave. Karlson piloted back as Karl instructed him in the rules for flying. Since Star People were the only ones in the air, except for birds of course, the rules were simple and few. Karl even let the boy pilot when they flew to school in the morning and home again in the afternoon. Karlson became somewhat of a celebrity when the other kids saw him at the controls. Suddenly school wasn't such a chore anymore!

* * *

Cook Gio's duty tour was up and he would be leaving. The starship *Expedition* had arrived and was in orbit around the planet, and it was time for the starship *Searcher* to prepare to leave. Everyone who had quarters in their hotel attended a "going away party" for Gio. Even the new cook (his replacement) was there. He was very nice, as were all the Star People, but he was *no* Gio.

Everyone would miss Gio, but especially Karlson. Gio was his buddy! He gave him really good treats, even before mealtimes. He helped with homework while preparing the dinner buffet. He taught him how to do stuff in the kitchen. He wasn't even mad when the dishes broke! He was a great guy, and everyone was sorry to see him go. And to make matters worse, they all started eating in the dining room instead of the kitchen—it was the new cook's idea.

This started Karlson thinking. Gio left to go to the Star People's home planet. He remembered that his dad had said that he would also be leaving to go home when his job here was done, and that his son would be going with him. He wondered what that would be like ... he wondered a lot.

Chapter 11

Little Monkeys

The school teachers of Karlson's class wanted to take their students to the zoo that had just opened in the next city. It would have been over a two hour trip to and then two hours back in the school bus, so they asked for assistance from the Star People. Happy to help out, Commander Karl obtained permission from the High Commander, and they prepared for the field trip. Karlson had never heard of a zoo before, and was fascinated with the idea. It was to be very exciting, as they were to go in a transport! Karlson was the center of attention at school as he explained about the transport that they would be taking, and how it flew so fast high up in the sky.

*

The day finally came! All the kids were very excited as they waited to board the great shining ship. Karlson was acting like a tour director, as if he alone was in charge of the 30 or so kids and several teachers.

Karl had invited Star Lady Alana to join them. Karlson just rolled his eyes. He figured that his dad would probably ignore him, as seemed to be the case every time she was there. But it would be OK this time, since there would be so much for him to do.

Everyone climbed the steps up to the entrance of the transport, entered, and took a seat. Alana sat next to Karl, naturally. Karlson sat up front with the teachers. All the kids were looking about and whispering with one another, awed with the luxury of the ship. When the door was sealed, they lifted off the field. The kids stretched in their seats to peer out the window viewports, to see the land below whiz by.

In no time at all, they were landing in the empty parking lot outside the zoo. A man who worked at the zoo met them as they exited the big transport. The three teachers reminded the kids to stay close and not wander off. They all walked together under the big zoo sign and into the high walled interior.

All week before, they had been studying the different kinds of animals that they might encounter at the zoo, so the kids were familiar with many. Just inside the fancy main building, there was a huge cage full of colorful birds that squawked loudly at them. There were lots of other cages too. The zoo worker walked with them, telling about the animals within each. Then they went outside, where they passed one large enclosure after another (a few stunk pretty bad). The zoo worker also explained that many of the animals had been brought there from other zoos. Because of the plague, there were few people left to properly care for them, so they needed new homes. In fact, a new shipment of small monkeys was due to arrive that very day.

After the tour, everyone received a drink in a cup with animal pictures all over it, plus a curly straw. As they were enjoying their drinks, the zoo worker got a call on his radio. The new shipment of monkeys had arrived. He offered to let the kids come and watch them being unloaded into their new home. The teachers agreed, so off they went.

They walked through the main zoo building and then out to another building where a big truck had backed up into a loading dock. This building was different from the first. This one was not very fancy at all, and the workers in there wore white lab coats. It was more like a big doctor's office, rather than part of the zoo. They all walked down a hall that had a rail on one side and was open to a big room. Large cages were being brought in as the truck was unloaded. The zoo man explained that these monkeys were from one of the few cities where the plague was still actively being fought.

Everyone thought it would be fun to see the monkeys, but it was actually quite frightening. The monkeys were crazed within their cages. They were screeching and baring their razor-sharp snapping teeth. Their slobber was flipping out everywhere. Their eyes were large with insane fury. They hung from the insides of their cages, jumping up and down, and tried to reach through the metal bars to grab anything they could. Even the people in the doctor room seemed afraid of them.

The zoo man explained that once each of the monkeys had been examined for any illness, they would be let go into a tunnel that led to the monkey enclosure, where they would enjoy a happy life.

Karl asked, "Is this type of monkey normally so aggressive?"

"No," the zoo man admitted. "This type is highly intelligent and usually quite gentle. They were always my favorite species. I really don't know what's wrong with them right now."

No sooner had he said that, one of the cages being carried into the room fell to the floor and popped open. Suddenly screeching monkeys were everywhere! The girls screamed, and so did the boys. The panicked children ran in all directions. The teachers tried to herd them into a side room. They got a number of kids in before having to slam the door in the faces of three viciously snarling monkeys. Several other kids were trapped down the hall. They threw their cups at the screeching monkeys and the flying ice seemed to scare them off enough for Alana to grab a broom and beat them back and away from the scared kids. She kept swinging the broom, forcing the monkeys away until she and the frightened kids reached the door to the room where the other children and teachers were. She quickly opened the door and shoved the kids inside. Then she slammed the door shut, and continued beating the broom at the monkeys.

Karl was protecting a larger group of terrified kids that were cornered. He hollered and kicked at the howling beasts, and even punched a few with his fists as they got too close. Alana continued beating her broom at the monkeys, pushing them back as she worked her way to Karl.

Karlson could see that the Star Lady was no wimp. He was a little bit ashamed of himself as he balanced his body quite safely on top of an open door. Several monkeys had tried to jump up at him, but couldn't quite make it so they went to torment elsewhere. He watched as one of the monkeys scurried to the other cages that were rocking back and forth with their enraged occupants inside. He began opening them! These monkeys *were* smart! Two of the people in the white lab coats lay on the floor, bleeding. When the smart monkey got one cage open, he went to the others to open them as well. Some of the newly freed beasts attacked the two injured people already down on the floor!

Alana had now reached Karl and the trapped kids, smashing her broom up and down, and yelling at the ferocious jumping monkeys. She and his dad would not be able to hold them off much longer as more and more monkeys were being set loose. Karlson felt that he had to do something. He saw another broom off to the side in the monkey room. He quickly calculated the distance and made his move. He slid down the door and dropped to the floor. He raced to the broom and then turned to smash it at the monkeys that were biting to death the two people on the floor. Seeing something more interesting than the unmoving bodies, they glared at Karlson for an instant before they attacked him!

Karlson could hear his dad yelling for him to get out of there, but he had a plan. He beat the broom at his attackers while backing toward the tunnel door to the monkey enclosure beyond. He passed by a bag of what appeared to be some sort of monkey food, so he grabbed it and quickly dumped some on the floor. That instantly got the attention of the monkeys, as they eagerly ate it up. He could still hear his dad shouting for him to get back on top of the door. More of the monkeys came to eat. For a moment they seemed to forget about Karlson, so he slid the door open to the tunnel and ducked inside. He dropped more food as he hunched over and ran down the narrow tunnel. He could hear them coming behind him, scrambling to gobble the food. He ran to the end of the tunnel ... but it was closed! He lay down on his back and kicked as hard as he could. The wooden door splintered and cracked, then thankfully it popped open.

He could hear a monkey right behind him. He rolled over and dumped more food from the bag. He then slipped through the broken tunnel door and hopped down into the monkey pit. His eyes adjusted to the bright sunlight and he quickly looked around. He was trapped! There were just tall slick walls all around except for a double wall of bars for people to watch the monkeys through. He could climb, but there was nowhere to climb to! He could dump all the food out into a pile and wait for the monkeys to come out and then sneak back into the tunnel ... but no, he couldn't be sure that more monkeys wouldn't still be in the tunnel and then get him.

By now, monkeys were pouring out of the broken tunnel door. He quickly dumped all the food out of the bag and ran away from it. He hoped that most of the monkeys would come after the food so his dad and everyone else could escape.

There was a big rock pile in the center of the pit, so Karlson had no choice but to climb it. He realized that there was no escape from the top of it, but maybe he could hold them off and then they would lose interest and go away.

He was halfway up when the monkey food ran out, and they turned their attention back to him. Even though he was once called "Little Monkey" because he could climb well and quickly, these were *real* monkeys and they were much faster. They leapt from one rock to another, closing the distance to him with amazing speed. He frantically climbed the remaining rocks to the very top. He sat there, as he watched them come closer and closer. Their eyes were full of crazed hatred. They snapped their sharp teeth together, as if practicing for the kill. Karlson kicked at them, wishing he still had the broom. One of them locked its teeth onto his shoe, but he kicked it in the face with his other foot and it let go.

He was really scared now. More and more were climbing up the rock pile to him. There were monkeys everywhere! What could he do? There weren't any small rocks up there to throw at them. All he had were his feet to kick with. He kept thinking ... *Dad told me to get back on top of the door, where I was safe, but I didn't. I disobeyed. Dad is really going to kill me if I die.*

Then a shadow came over him. The monkeys began jumping back down. What was going on? He looked up to see the huge transport just above him. It was almost more frightening looking than the monkeys! A long knotted strap was lowered down from the open hatch high above. It got closer and closer to where Karlson could grab it. He reached out and his fingers barely touched it, but he couldn't catch it. It swung away, but then swung back again in his direction. This time he got it! He hung on and hollered to the unseen people above. The transport slowly moved upward and Karlson hung tightly to the strap as he swung around in mid air. It was actually pretty easy, and kind of fun. He watched the ground move away as he was hauled upward. He slid along the shiny smooth metal of the transport side and then was suddenly at the open hatch door. His dad pulled him in and they both fell back into the ship.

"I'm so mad at you!" Karl said as he hugged the boy tightly.

"Dad, I can't breathe!" Karlson gasped.

Karl loosened his hug, and they both laughed.

The lady Alana hugged him too. She was very soft and smelled like strawberry ice cream. He really couldn't blame his dad for liking her.

*

A few days later, the zoo people called Commander Karl. It turned out that the monkeys actually had contracted the plague, but instead of it killing them, it made them crazy. They were given the vaccine, and it cured them all; they were again docile and friendly. The zoo offered another visit to the school children. When the teachers asked the kids if they wanted a return visit to the zoo, no hands went up. No, not even one.

Chapter 12

Leaving

The time had come. Karl was scheduled to leave his post as Commander of Sector Seven. Everyone whose duty tour was up—and that included just about everyone who had originally arrived on the starship *Seeker*—would be leaving for the two month voyage back to the Star People's home planet.

On the morning of departure, Karlson packed all his possessions into two bags that his dad had gotten for him. He and Karl said goodbye to all those who were staying behind, with promises to get together when they were all back home again.

That afternoon they took a flyer to the landing field. Karl carried his bags plus one of Karlson's bags and deposited them on the big trolley that would go into the cargo area of the transport. Karlson plopped his bag down on it as well, but it slid off, so Karl had to heave it up for him. Then they boarded the "big egg" transport, but this time *every* seat was soon filled, and, with all the talking and laughing, it was anything but quiet.

Within half an hour, they took off. Karlson had no sense of loss as he watched his world shrink slowly in the distance. It had been a hard existence for such a young boy. He was excited and eager to begin a new chapter in his life as a Star Man's Son aboard a Star People spaceship, going to the Star People world.

They arrived at the *Seeker* and received their quarter assignments. Karl had arranged to have the boy assigned a room right next to his in the officer's section. Karlson was glad, as it had never occurred to him that they might be separated.

*

Karlson was doing very well in learning the Star People language, but he was surprised when his dad said that they would be speaking *only* in that language during the two month voyage. His dad said it was the best way for him to learn quickly and correctly. It was a bit of a pain, but he understood more and was able to speak better each day that passed. It was learning to *write* the language that really was a huge problem! He had barely mastered reading and writing in his *own* language, and now he had to learn another!

There wasn't much to do on the long trip. In addition to his writing lessons and mealtimes, he played checkers with crewmembers in the lounge. His dad mounted his dart board in the lounge as well, so everyone could play. (He had packed his toys and games in the luggage bags as well as his clothes—but not the bike, which he had to sadly leave behind.)

When he wasn't doing his lessons, and no one was around to play darts or checkers, he would explore the ship. There were lots of hallways running the length of the "bun," all parallel to each other. For instance, if you opened a hotdog bun and ran lots of lines of ketchup from one end of the bun to the other, and then put the hotdog in and closed the bun over it ... those ketchup lines would be the linear hallways.

Then there were the "belly-band" hallways (the crew had nicknamed them). These six hallways went around the circumference of the ship—like if you put six rubber bands spaced apart around the "bun," with one around the front, and continuing with the last one at the back. Those passages (on the inside of the bun, of course!) allowed someone to walk from one starting point in one direction and go all around the entire "bun" and end up right back at the same starting point. Karlson walked them all. He also walked the many long linear halls from the front to the back of the ship, jumping from one to the next via a belly-band hallway.

There were also many sets of stairs that went up to the decks above. His dad explained it to him. Each deck was like a cylinder— a long tube—and all of these deck cylinders surrounded the hub as one big rotating unit. The other side of the floor of deck A was the outer skin of the ship. On the other side of the ceiling of deck A, was the floor of deck B, and the other side of the ceiling of deck B, was the floor of deck C, and so on. The outermost deck A was the largest, and deck F was the smallest (because it had the least diameter of its cylindrical shape) and closest to the hub (the "hotdog"). There were also elevators that ran from the outer deck A up to and through the other inner decks surrounding the hub.

Each of those decks also had long linear hallways and "belly-bands" too. On deck A, the floor seemed flat everywhere, but on the upper decks, his dad had said, you could actually see the curvature of the floor ahead of where you were walking in a belly-band hallway.

Most everything "people" related—living quarters, offices, control room, science labs, dining, lounges and such—were on deck A, where gravity was normal. On deck B, there was a weapons range, a gymnasium, and other things that Karlson did not know what the names meant. Decks C, D, and E were for storage of the massive amounts of supplies a starship needed. On each deck, the closer it was to the hub, the less gravity it had. Deck F was the closest deck to the center hub of the ship. Deck G (the hub—which was not actually a deck at all) was the "hotdog" or the zero-gravity chamber—the Dead Zone. Karlson was not allowed to go to any of those decks above B.

*

Meal times were always fun. Everyone liked the boy with his neatly cut straight dark hair—even those who secretly thought that a starship was no place for a child. He was polite, courteous, respectful, and always eager to learn. He also made them laugh when he got their language wrong. Not even a week had passed when, instead of a stool at the dinner table, he was surprised to find a tall chair there, with a seat that fit his body perfectly! The crewmen in "Maintenance/Construction" had made it for him. The next day, he went to that section and thanked them all.

*

One night at dinner, the Captain of the ship joined them, and Karlson peppered him with questions: How fast does the ship go? How do you turn the ship? Has the ship ever bumped into anything? After those and about 20 more questions like that, the Captain invited him to come visit the control room the next day. Karl, surprised by the invitation, nodded his approval. Karlson could hardly wait!

The next morning after breakfast, Karlson joined the Captain and the bridge crew. Each of the bridge officers was very kind and showed the eager boy what they did at their stations. The Captain even let him place a routine call to headquarters. (They were quite shocked to hear a child's small voice!) He asked if he could come back sometime to see if he could remember everything that he had learned. The Captain promised a return invitation in the future. That evening at dinner he was a total chatterbox, telling everyone at the table what he had seen. They all acted interested, in spite of already being completely familiar with everything he described.

Everyone liked the innocent enthusiasm of the boy.

100

*

Two weeks into the voyage, a call came in. It was an order for the *Seeker* to go and investigate why another starship, the *Adventurer*, had lost contact with everyone. The *Seeker* was the closest ship to the last known position of the *Adventurer*, so there was no choice in the matter. It would take two months to get there and another two months to return back to their original course. Everyone was disappointed to have their journey home interrupted and lengthened, but no one complained.

*

Intrigued by the idea of just floating around in zero-gravity, Karlson asked his dad if they could go to the Dead Zone. Karl said yes, so they went. As they walked down the hallway, Karlson asked a very intelligent question. "I don't understand how anything can *not* weigh something. Maybe a feather or air doesn't weigh much, but I do, and you do, so how can we possibly ever be 'weightless'?"

"That's a very good question, son, and one that some folks have difficulty understanding. The confusion comes with the difference between weight and *mass*. Mass is the body of something. You have mass. I have more mass than you. A feather has mass but less mass than you. Even air has mass. But weight is the effect gravity has *upon* that mass. The more gravity, the more weight. We are going to a zero-gravity zone where you still have mass, but there will be no gravity to pull on you, so you will be weightless."

Karl paused, "What do you think it would be like if you were in a *high* gravity situation, higher than a planet's natural gravity that we're used to?"

The boy thought a moment, "We would be so heavy that we could hardly move?"

"Very good!" His dad smiled. "You've got it!"

As they walked on, Karl warned his son that some people did not like zero-gravity, as it made them sick in their stomachs. Karl himself did not particularly like it, but he could handle it.

They came to the first set of stairs. Karl explained that as they went up, the gravity—centrifugal throw—caused by the rotation of the ship's hull, would become less and less. When they reached C deck, it was quite noticeable. Karlson felt like he could jump five feet up in the air, but his father warned him not to because he wasn't used to it. It wasn't the jump that was the problem, it was the landing ... he might go splat into the wall!

When they reached E deck, they were light enough that Karlson thought he might just be able to fly! Neither one of them felt sick, so up they continued to the sixth deck, F, where they were nearly weightless. F deck wasn't really much of a deck at all; it was just the staging place to enter G deck—the Dead Zone. Karl explained that in the zero-gravity chamber, there was no rotation because it was at the center—the hub—which extended from the front end of the ship all the way to the back end—and the ship's massive body turned around it.

"The hotdog!" Karlson interjected.

"Yes," his dad chuckled. "Exactly."

Karl explained that before entering the chamber, everyone must wear a mag-belt, which went around the waist. When turned on, it would energize the electromagnet within the belt, and cause the wearer to float toward the metal wall of the zero-gravity chamber. Karl also explained that there were little compartments all over the zero chamber which contained bags ... to use if you suddenly *do* become sick!

They put on the mag-belts; Karl had to wrap it three times around Karlson's thin waist.

"Ready?"

Karlson nodded eagerly, "Let's go!"

They waited for the opening to appear. Because the entire ship was rotating around the center hub tube—the zero gravity Dead Zone (which was *not* rotating)—there were openings spaced all along it for entrance into it. One could not waste time entering the opening when it appeared, because the ship's entire hull continued to turn around the stationary hub, and the opening would soon close. It was fairly slow moving, but still, if you didn't move fast enough, you would be cut in half if the turning "bun" closed the opening to the Dead Zone before you were all the way in ... maybe that's another reason they called it the *Dead* Zone.

As the opening appeared and grew large enough, they grabbed the hand-hold bars at the hatch doorway and then swung themselves in through the opening into the Dead Zone.

It was so weird! They both just hung in mid air. They were floating!

Then Karl said to the giggling boy, "Let go of the bar."

Karl held the boy's arm and moved him out away from the wall—and then he let go. "Try to come back to me," he said mischievously to the boy.

Karlson reached, but did not move. He kicked his feet, but did not move. He tried swimming, but *still* he did not move.

By then Karl was laughing at the boy's predicament. "Son, you are in *zero* gravity! No amount of struggling will make you move unless you have something to push off of ... or you have a mag-belt. Turn it on like I showed you."

Karlson found the switch on the belt and turned it on. Gradually he floated toward the metal wall. "That is why we must wear the mag-belts. It is a safety rule. Like you know now, it's real easy to let go of a hold bar and end up just floating about, with no way to get out of it."

Then Karlson had fun. Karl had turned on the lights, and they could see all the way from one far away end of the zero chamber to the other. They were inside the "hotdog!" Everywhere along the walls there were red colored hold bars—for hands but also large enough for feet. You could hold yourself against the curved wall (which was also the floor) with the toe of your shoe, then push off and float down the long cylinder of the zero gravity chamber. It was like flying! The harder you pushed off, the faster you went. If you angled your push, you would float-fly to the wall down a bit, and then push off again and float-fly to another spot. (You just had to avoid an opening that was being opened or closed as the ship rotated.) Karlson even did somersaults but was quickly warned by his dad to not overdo it.

Karlson had a great time.

Chapter 13

The Array

Karlson had so much fun in the Dead Zone that he pestered his father to go often. Each time they went, Karlson did not have to be reminded to put on his mag-belt, and he handled himself safely in the zone. So, after a while, Karl let him go by himself as long as he asked for permission first.

Alone in the Zone!

One day, as he was perfecting his back flips, he heard voices. He was *not* alone in the zone! He pushed off firmly and "flew" down the long cylindrical chamber to a group of men at the very front end.

"Hi!" the boy shouted.

Two of the three men nearly jumped out of their skins! "Whoa! Don't sneak up on us like that again! Thought you were a ghost or something."

"Sorry!" Karlson said, trying not to smile at how the big Star Men had been so startled.

The third man was laughing. "You guys get spooked easily."

"Well, it's creepy in here."

"The sooner we're out of this place, the better."

"What are you doing in here, boy?" the unspooked crewman asked.

"My dad lets me come up here to ... work out."

"The gym's better, if you ask me."

"Yes, but this is much more fun!" Karlson said brightly.

"If you think so," the crewman laughed.

Karlson watched as they flipped two lock levers and opened the hatch to the forward dome. He thought to himself—this must be the front end of the "hotdog," the part that sticks out of the "bun."

He could hear a strange sound, so he asked politely, "Sir, what is that noise?"

"What noise?"

"Oh, I think he means the hull rotation gears," said another. "That sound is the gearing mechanism that allows the main part of the ship to turn around the stationary hub—this long zero-gravity cylinder that runs the length of the entire ship. There are seven sets of rotation gears and motors positioned along the hub—for a smooth and even rotation. The rotation causes a centrifugal force, a kind of artificial gravity, for all the decks ... do you understand?"

"Yes, sir, I do. My dad explained it to me."

"You just have to avoid being sliced and diced, when the openings close," one of the other crewmen said.

"Yes, sir, I know. I go through as quickly as I can."

They returned to their job, consulting a set of schematics (drawings) of the positions of many very powerful cameras that made up the forward visuals. The three men pushed themselves into the nose section where the hundreds of outward pointed cameras and other sensors were all arranged around the inside of the clear dome.

This must be the array. Karlson thought to himself. Here is the sensor equipment that the ship needs, like cameras, radar, radio, and stuff.

"It's camera 28," one man said as he referred to the maintenance request.

"Camera 28 ... it's in section 2 ... green," the crewman holding the schematic said.

"Yes, I see it," the crewman closest to the problem replied, and then asked, "Give me the screwdriver, please."

One of the others reached into the tool bag and pulled a power driver off the magnetic holding strip. He gave it a little push, and it floated into the other man's waiting hand. Using the battery operated screwdriver, he quickly opened the cover panel. He stuck his head in and found camera 28. He put his arm in too but couldn't quite reach it. "Can't get to it," he sighed with frustration. "We're going to have to take the whole assembly out. The ship will be partially blind for about an hour ... Captain won't like it."

Karlson, still quietly watching from the hatch, caught the maintenance request form that had drifted away from the man who had gotten the tool out.

"Here," Karlson said as he handed the paper back. "This was getting away."

"Thanks," he said, then immediately exclaimed, "What about the boy? Can he fit in the hole?"

The two other men stared at Karlson. "You know, he just might fit."

Then he asked the boy, "Can you help us out? One of the cameras has gone out and we need to replace it."

"Sure!" Karlson said, eager to help.

He slipped through the hatch and entered the large dome. He looked about but couldn't see much through the clear curved surface of the dome, because of all the equipment. He floated over to the open panel.

"Look in here," the man pointed.

Karlson stuck his head through the open panel hole.

"See the camera housings in there? See the green one?"

Karlson saw many colored things in there, including several green ones.

"It's the one to your left and up."

"I think I see it," the boy replied.

"Good, let me show you what to do."

Karlson pulled his head out of the hole and the crewman explained how to pop the green guard piece up and then remove the defective camera, replace it with the new one, then close the guard. Simple. They stuffed the new camera in his pocket, and back into the hole he went, all the way in nearly to his feet.

"See the green one? Do you see '28' on it?"

"Yes, sir."

"Pop the guard off and pull out the camera."

"Got it!"

"Now, take the new camera out of your pocket and just before you put it in, pull the protective lens cover off, and be careful *not* to touch the lens as you push it in! Any kind of oil from your fingertips will mess up the lens."

The men waited breathlessly for a few moments.

"It's in!"

"Great, kid! Now push down the green guard until you hear it snap."

"Done!"

They carefully pulled Karlson out of the hole and thanked him profusely. He had saved them much time and the ship visuals were not going to be disturbed—which would please the Captain.

Karlson gave them the defective camera and lens protector, and said, "Anytime you need my help, just let me know!"

The men laughed and promised him they would.

* * *

Karl began to notice that Karlson's pants were looking a bit short on his growing legs, plus some of his shirts seemed to be fitting more snugly. He hadn't thought to bring larger clothing sizes for the boy as he had not expected to spend more time in space, other than the original trip home. So, one morning they took a walk to an area of the ship called "Ship Services." They entered and found a room with the sign "Tailoring" over the door. Karl walked over and leaned on the higher part of the counter. "Hello!" he said smiling at the woman sitting at a desk.

Seeing the handsome officer, she flashed him a flirty smile, "Hello, Commander!"

Karlson, noticing her interest in his dad, looked at the woman … why, she looked old enough to be his dad's mother … no—his *grand*mother!

"My boy needs some clothes, especially pants. We didn't expect to be on an extended mission, so we didn't bring any larger sizes for him. He nodded down at Karlson. "He's growing like a weed!"

She got up and moved to the lower counter, where Karlson stood. She peered at him over her glasses. "Hmm, I don't really have much in the way of civilian cloth, mostly just extra uniform fabric."

Karl said, "Actually a uniform will work just fine. He'll be going to the Academy when we get home."

She smiled sweetly at Commander Karl. Then she looked the boy up and down. "Well, I don't have the makings for a *cadet* uniform either, but I think I could alter a small standard officer's uniform to fit him."

She invited the boy to come behind the counter and then she measured him. "You *both* come back in a few days, and we'll have a fitting."

They thanked her and left. He was going to get to wear a uniform just like his dad!

*

When they came back, the woman had Karlson put on something that didn't look like a uniform at all! It was pieces and more pieces of fabric that were put together with tape. He must have looked worried because the woman assured him that she wasn't finished with it yet. She made some minor changes with the tape, and then told them both to come back in a few more days, smiling at handsome Commander Karl all the while.

*

They came back as instructed, and Karlson was presented with a complete uniform—just like all the officers wore! But it was much, much smaller, and very plain; it didn't have any shiny insignia on it. The lady was very pleased with the fit. She said she was sorry that she couldn't do anything about proper boots, because they just didn't have any sized that small, but the rest of the uniform was perfect! Both Karl and Karlson thanked her profusely. She said she would have more made and sent to them, unless of course, Commander Karl wanted to come pick them up—personally. She smiled at him dreamily.

As they were walking down the hall, Karlson looked up. "Dad," he grinned, "I think she *likes* you!"

After a moment, a small teasing smile curled Karl's lips, "Well, can you blame her?"

Never having heard or seen any type of arrogance or vanity whatsoever from his dad, Karlson knew he was joking, so they both laughed.

Chapter 14

Ghost Ship

After two months travel, they easily found the *Adventurer*. The ship was exactly at the given coordinates of its last known position. It was stopped in space, high above a lifeless planet. They radioed the ship, but got no response.

Commander Karl and one other officer, in a mini-shuttle, toured the *Adventurer's* outer hull. The ship's skin looked intact, with no evidence of any damage. They returned to the *Seeker* with their report. Then another group went to the *Adventurer* in a larger shuttle and docked. They entered and searched the ship but saw no one. They broadcasted on the full ship-wide intercom, but there was no response. They read the ship's log, but found nothing to explain the weird absence of the entire crew. They decided to stay the night, just in case they were missing something.

The next morning, there were still no answers.

Karl went with a second group over to the silent ship. The team leader decided to send a shuttle to the surface of the planet to a place where the missing crew had been exploring. He didn't see how they could *all* be there, because all the ship's transports were still onboard, but he wished to examine every possibility.

Everyone on the *Seeker* was talking about the "ghost" ship. All kinds of fanciful theories and explanations were tossed about, but none seemed logical. Karlson waited for his father to return. He was full of mixed emotions. He wasn't *really* worried about his dad's safety on a ghost ship (well, maybe just a little), but he was anxious for his return. Plus, he was curious ... a ghost ship!

He dared to think of an idea. Both the Captain and the High Commander had thanked him for his help in fixing the broken camera in the forward array ... so maybe ... just maybe ....

*

Karlson gathered his courage and knocked on the High Commander's door.

"Enter!"

Karlson opened the door and saluted.

"At ease, son, what do you want to see me for?"

"Sir, I respectfully request your permission to join my dad on the *Adventurer*."

"Why?" the High Commander said bluntly.

Karlson wasn't expecting that. He thought quickly, "I ... I think it would be a good learning experience, sir."

"And it might be fun too, eh?" The High Commander tried to hide his smile.

"Uh, yes sir, I ... yes, sir."

"I've been told that you've been doing very well in your studies—especially in learning our language. And I agree that any new experience can be a learning experience, as long as reasonable caution is taken. So, young man, permission to join the *Adventurer* crew is granted. Report to Crewman Jenner in 'Suit Maintenance' at the hangar deck. Dismissed!"

Karlson executed another perfect salute, turned smartly, and left. As he shut the door behind him, he could hardly believe how easy that was!

Karlson checked the ship directory on an information screen that could be found on just about every wall in the ship. He easily found the hangar deck and was directed off to the side to a section named "Suit Maintenance." He found Crewman Jenner in "Pressure Suit Storage"—a room where they kept a large number of space suits. Jenner was going through one after another when he saw Karlson. Karlson snapped a crisp salute, but before he could say anything, Jenner smiled, "It's OK, you don't have to salute me. 'High' called down a few minutes ago and told me to expect you. We need to find you a suit! I know there should be some smaller ones here," he mumbled as he slid one bright white suit after another down a heavy rail from which they were hanging. "Ah, here we go!" He lifted one off the rail and held it up to Karlson. He shook his head. "Still a might large. Let's see what we can do about that."

"Am I going to wear a space suit over there on the *Adventurer*?"

"We call it a pressure suit, and no, both the shuttle and that ship are pressurized, but no one goes on a mission in space without a suit onboard their ride. It's a requirement—for safety, you know."

Karlson watched as Crewman Jenner manipulated the heavy suit fabric—bunching it under adjustable straps on each leg. Then he did the same on the arms.

"Let's give that a try."

He helped Karlson into the suit, explaining how to attach the huge gloves. The boots were way too big, but they would have to do. He turned Karlson toward a full length mirror so the boy could see how to attach the clear-front "bubble" helmet.

Karlson stared at himself in the mirror. The bunching of fabric at the straps made his legs and arms "poof" out unnaturally. This was the first time—ever—that he looked fat!

Karlson thanked Crewman Jenner, and clumsily carried his very own pressure suit—complete with his name that Jenner had put on the front, back, and even on the helmet. It was heavy! As he was directed by Crewman Jenner, he walked over to hangar Bay 10 toward the waiting shuttle. Hangar bays were like giant garages for space craft. He entered the small shuttle ship, and stowed his suit where he was told. Then he sat down and waited. Several minutes passed until the last of the scheduled crew arrived.

Suddenly bright red lights flashed on and off, and loud alarms sounded as the heavy airtight hangar door behind their craft slowly lowered to the deck. When it was completely shut, he could then hear the whining sound of the pumps as they removed the air from the small hangar bay. Suddenly the big doors in front cracked open to the vast darkness of space. He pressed his face to the viewport as the great doors slowly opened fully. This was different from the trips he had taken on the large transport to and from his planet's surface. This was a bit scary!

As their craft lifted off the hangar deck and slowly slipped into the emptiness of space, he peered all around. The great starship was behind them, and getting smaller by the seconds, but he could see nothing else. Then, it seemed like a star in the distance ahead began to grow. It continued to grow until he could see that it wasn't a star at all, but a duplicate of the ship they had just left. The Ghost Ship! After a few more minutes, they landed inside a bay that looked exactly like the one they had just left. The big space doors closed and then they waited for the hangar to re-pressurize before disembarking.

Karl was waiting at the hangar. He was glad to see the boy, as he knew it would be a nice break from his studies and possibly a new adventure for him. He was also impressed that his son had the initiative and courage to go to the High Commander and ask for permission ... and even more surprised that the High Commander gave it!

*

Other than the air smelling a bit different, being on the *Adventurer* was just the same as being on the *Seeker*—except that there was no one there, other than the crew members from their ship. Karlson accompanied his dad to the control room, where he had been recording information. It looked just like the control room on the *Seeker*. He did not need to be told not to touch anything. Ahead was the huge viewscreen showing the planet before them. It was a reddish color, with white at the poles. He was seeing another world!

Karl interrupted his mesmerized son, "Keep looking, the twin moons will come into view soon." No sooner than he had said that—there they were! Two bright orbs!

Karlson intelligently asked, "Why are they so close together? Wouldn't they bump into each other?"

"Yes, we always thought so, until now. We really don't know how they can exist in such close proximity to each other—without their gravitational pulls causing them to crash together. We always thought that the rules of gravity were ... finite. Come here ... see this dial? It adjusts the viewscreen." He turned the dial on the colorful control panel and the view of the planet and the moons grew instantly larger. They could see the rough craters on one of the moons. On the other, the surface seemed smooth. They could also see the red planet much better, but the closer the view, the less red it became—it seemed to turn more brownish.

Karl moved a lever next to the magnification dial. A glowing dot appeared on the screen. He moved it across the viewscreen to a point over the surface of the planet. "That's where the rest of our team went. It's the place where this ship's daily logs indicated they had been exploring. I hope we find them there, or at least get some answers."

Karl finished getting the information he needed, and with some time left, he put it to good use. He showed Karlson how different things in the control room operated. He started with the magnification dial, letting Karlson set it back to "neutral" plus turning the location dot to "off." Much of it the boy remembered from his previous visit to the control room on the *Seeker*.

Karl watched his son as he explained things. The boy absorbed everything like a sponge. He was so eager to learn, and had an amazing intellect to understand and remember. Karl suspected that his son had a substantially above-average I.Q.

*

They were preparing to leave the control room, and Karlson was casually looking toward the open exit door. Suddenly, something nearly transparent crossed in the hallway outside the door! He momentarily wasn't sure whether he actually saw something or not. He slowly walked through the door and into the hall. There! He saw it again! It was a man—and not one from their ship. Our uniforms were blue, but that one was silver. The man was walking toward him, and then he faded into nothingness!

Karlson was stunned. After he gulped several times, he stammered, "D-Dad ... do you believe in g-ghosts?"

"Son, from the crazy stuff I've seen so far, I'll believe in just about anything, but why do you ask?"

"I saw a man. He was just there and then he ... disappeared! He was a ... he was a g-ghost!" Karlson stammered.

"You saw a man? One of us?"

"No, sir, he had on a silver uniform, not blue. Then he just disappeared!" Karlson pointed. "Right there!"

The boy wasn't a silly prankster, so Karl knew he had seen *something*. They both went into the hallway, and after carefully looking into each of the rooms along it, found nothing. They continued down the hall toward a "belly-band" hallway that branched off theirs. Suddenly, a figure appeared ahead, then instantly disappeared!

"Whoa!" Karl exclaimed.

They both ran toward the spot where the hallways crossed. The apparition was gone. Then, there it was again, walking away from them! Karlson was frozen with apprehension, but his brave dad ran up to it and then passed it! He walked backwards before the oncoming "ghost." He was talking to it, but it did not seem to notice him at all; it just kept walking until it faded again from existence. Karl pushed the radio button on his uniform, and reported what they had seen. Shortly, the rest of the team arrived at their location.

*

For the next hour, the team conferred by video with the scientists on the *Seeker*, with the Captain and High Commander listening in. By then, several others had seen ghosts as well. They reviewed all the facts. The ghosts had to be the crew of the *Adventurer*. They seemed to be unaware of the *Seeker* crew-member presence on their ship. Theories were discussed. The *Adventurer* crew seemed alive, but were "out of phase" somehow with normal space and time. They were perhaps slipping in and out of our dimension. The big questions were, of course, how to determine what was causing it and to find a way to get them back. But there was risk. What if whatever had caused this might cause them *also* to fall into the ghostly limbo? There was concern about the risk, but no dissent. Being the honorable people that they were, they decided to do whatever was necessary to help—whatever the risks.

The team was called back from the surface of the planet (they hadn't found anything anyway) and groups of two were assigned to search the entire ship—this time looking for anything weird or unusual. Karl and his son were assigned to the engine room.

*

Karl and Karlson made their way to the engine room at the far rear of the massive ship. Karlson felt lighter, so he jumped a little. Sure enough, his jump was higher than twice of what he normally could. The engine room was located around the center of the ship's end, encompassing the rear area of decks B, C, D, E, and F— but all open as one great room. It was the biggest place that Karlson had ever seen on a starship! Great machinery of the star-drive engines reached all the way to the ceiling. Being that it was an inner deck of the ship, they could see the curvature of the floor under their feet, even though it felt level to them as they walked. Karlson studied the oddly curved "ceiling" as they walked and realized that it was the cylindrical tube that ran all the way from the front array to the rear of the ship where they were. It was the center hub, and inside it was one of his favorite places—the Dead Zone, but at the far back end of it.

They searched for a couple of hours, but found nothing amiss. Karlson looked into a small room labeled "Power Modulation" above the door. He looked up and down, and behind the open door. (You always should look behind a door, everyone knows that. That's where scary things might hide.) He saw nothing, turned back with a quick glance around the room, and was about to leave when a small movement caught his sharp eyes. There was something there! He stood perfectly still and stared at it. It was a soft shimmer—a waviness—just hanging in the air. It was not connected to anything, it was just ... there. He continued to stare at it with almost hypnotic fascination, and then he slowly moved his pointing finger toward the glimmer.

"No! Don't touch it!" Karl's voice called out sharply behind him.

His mind cleared instantly and he jumped back.

Karl called in their find. They sent video back to the scientists on the *Seeker*. Soon others from their team came and took readings on the strange phenomenon, but their readings showed absolutely nothing there. After intense discussion, the prevailing theory was that this anomaly, this unknown "thing" (being the only oddity that their ship-wide search had turned up), was probably the cause of the problem ... possibly interacting with the star-drive power that was still engaged, but in neutral mode, and thus perhaps was interfering somehow with normal space/time.

The group was discussing how to proceed when someone whispered, "Look at Gabe!" They all turned to Crewman Gabe. He was transparent! As they watched with horror, he slowly phased back to normal. Gabe had come on the first boarding party to the stranded ship, and had remained there the entire time.

Karl, even though he was not the leader on this mission, issued the order over his radio. "Attention everyone! Every person who has been on this ship the entire time since our arrival, go immediately to your shuttle and prepare to leave!" He then called the team leader and told him what had just happened. He agreed with Karl's action. Their fears were proving true—the effect that held the *Adventurer* in its grasp was now going to get them too!

There was no time. If they stayed, the phase-time-dimension-whatever warp thing would trap them too. But what to do? They couldn't leave the ghostly crew the way they were—half-in and half-out of reality. What to do?

The scientists suggested trying to touch the "wavy air" with a non-conductive object, to see if it would react. So, they took a plastic writing pen and cautiously approached the shimmer. Then, ever so slowly, they passed the pen into it and through it. The thing did not react. How do you deal with something that appears not to be there—but still is? And how would they get this unreal thing off the ship? Time was running out. Everyone was thinking hard, but no answers were forthcoming.

Then, Karl had an idea. "Maybe we don't have to get it off the ship. Maybe we have to get the ship off *it!*"

Everyone stared at Commander Karl.

"It might be that this thing is stationary—stuck in its position. We don't dare use the star-drive, but we could move the ship with the mini thrusters. Move it just enough to see if that thing moves *with* the ship or remains in its position *irrelevant* to the ship!"

Everyone agreed that it was worth a try, since they were at a loss as to whatever else could be done. As a precaution, all the crewmembers of the *Seeker* were ordered into their shuttles except for one officer, a starship control room pilot. Before they left, they set up a video camera aimed at the strange shimmering thing, so that the pilot could watch it from the control room as he prepared to move the great ship.

Karl and Karlson returned to their original shuttles. They could not ride together because of the pressure suit rules, and there was no time to get one and then take it to the other. The shuttles launched and pulled away from the huge ship to, what they hoped, would be a safe distance. It seemed to take much longer, but it was just minutes as they all waited anxiously. The spilt picture on the viewscreen in each shuttle showed both the control room of the ghost ship and the shimmer thing in the power modulation room. Then, from their viewports they saw just one mini thruster fire—one short burst from its port. Even though they could not really discern it, the huge ship moved.

They all could see it on the split screen. The shimmer moved! No, actually it did *not* move—the ship around it moved. The theory worked! The "OK" was given to move the ship more, enough to hopefully clear the thing completely—leaving it in outer space. The mini thrusters fired once more, and the *Adventurer* moved again.

Everyone watched tensely as the shimmer gradually disappeared through the wall. The big ship continued to move far enough to thoroughly clear the strange thing, with much room to spare. Suddenly, people appeared in the control room! One man nearly jumped out of his skin when he saw the pilot from the *Seeker*—seemingly appearing out of thin air in front of *him*! They were back! They were all back!

The team leader's shuttle immediately went back to the *Adventurer* so they could tell the newly found crew what had happened. Karl and the others went back to the *Seeker*. After their shuttles docked, father and son together brought their pressure suits to be stored in the "Active Astronaut" locker room. When they left, Karlson's suit was hanging right next to his dad's.

*

As both starships prepared to move away from the dangerous anomaly, that area of space was carefully noted, and the information was then distributed by hyperspace radio to all the fleet's navigation information systems and star charts. Space warning beacons were set out, and the area was marked "Absolute Quarantine"—the strongest warning of all. Then the two ships moved further away from the strange shimmer ... about a million miles away, to be exact. Crew members visited between the two ships. It was quite a happy reunion for all and a mystifying story to discuss. The missing people were totally shocked at being told that, what they perceived to be several hours, was actually several months real time!

Many—probably all—thanked Karl personally for their rescue from what they described as a dream, a strange nightmare from which they could not awake. Karlson also got much attention for first spotting the dreadful thing that had trapped them. Karl hoped the attention wouldn't "go to his head." But he smiled to himself; his son had too much sense and self-discipline to let that happen.

*

When things settled down, Karl suggested that Karlson write a note to the High Commander, thanking him for the opportunity to go off-ship and join the team. Hand-writing a note was a bit old fashioned, but it showed educated polite manners.

As he was still learning to write in the Star People language, Karlson formed his letters carefully—practicing some words on scrap paper to get them right. He wrote: "Sir, Thank you for giving me permission to go to the *Adventurer*. It was a good teachering." He signed it and put the note into an envelope and delivered it to the High Commander's secretary.

A few days later, he got a note back! It read: "Our thanks to you for finding the anomaly. Your fine performance will be included in your permanent record. Keep up the good work, and I am sure you will one day become a superb Officer." It was signed by the High Commander.

Karlson couldn't stop smiling as he read it several times. After he showed it to his father, he put the note carefully away, but secretly looked at it often.

*

After a number of days, the two ships parted ways. The *Adventurer* went on to continue its original mission, and the *Seeker* did as well—to go home. The side trip to find the *Adventurer* had taken two months to get there, and would take two more months to return to their original course. Nothing much happened during that time except that the Captain had invited Karlson back to the control room as he had promised. The boy very much enjoyed learning how the complicated starship operated.

* * *

When the *Seeker* arrived back to its original course, Karlson was eager to learn all about his father's home, which was to be his new home as well. He looked at pictures of the Star People's planet. It had oceans and great masses of land just like his own home world. There were mountains, large inland lakes, farms, and cities—again similar to his world, except for the cities—they were much, much bigger and seemed more "new."

Everything was easy to understand except for the government history. His dad tried to explain. "Our civilization used to be diverse in cultures between land areas—like your home planet is now. Throughout our history, the people lived in various kinds of social systems. Some were in tyranny, where the rulers treated the people like slaves. Some were in freedom and liberty, where the people could do pretty much what they wanted, within the law.

"Our people finally realized that freedom was the key to increased creativity and technology advances like never seen before. So, now we have a system where we have maximum freedom but also along with maximum personal responsibility."

Karlson appeared confused. "What does that mean?"

"Well, our people realized that we *each* had to take responsibility for our *own* actions, instead of blaming anyone or anything else for them. Everyone has choices to make ... do the right thing or the wrong thing, do the selfish thing or the generous thing, do the honorable thing or the dishonorable thing ... and accept the consequences for those choices. Most of us use our freedom to make the right choices. Do you understand?"

"Yes, sir, I do. But aren't some things hard to decide which is right or wrong?"

"Sometimes," Karl agreed, "it can seem so. That's where mistakes can be made. But, if you take your time and think about it, you can usually decide on the right choice."

"Is that why the Star People decided to save my world from the plague, because it was the right thing to do?"

"Yes, we value life above all."

Karlson thought for a moment. "Are the Star People going to try to make my world like yours?"

"No, son, we try not to interfere like that. We might suggest and encourage, but we do not wish to take over. We were not there to take anything from your people or your world, only to help."

"But you could, couldn't you? Star People are very powerful and could do anything they wanted. If Star People were bad, they could be real mean and ...."

"No," Karl interrupted, "we would never want to be mean—not to anybody."

"I believe that," Karlson grinned, "because you don't have a mean bone in your body!"

Karl raised an eyebrow in amused surprise. "I never heard an expression like that before—but I like it!"

Chapter 15

New Mission

Shortly after they had resumed their original course to the Star People's home planet, another call came. New Orders: A strange and seemingly unnatural power surge was picked up by one of the powerful reporting buoys that had been sent into deep space. The *Seeker* was ordered to go investigate, and then remain to explore the distant area of previously unvisited space.

Everyone onboard, whose off-world duty tours were up, was offered a choice to sign on for two more years of off-world duty, or continue home and be substituted by new crewmembers. Karl wanted to see his family and friends back home, but he considered his son's welfare. The boy was still mastering the language, and certainly needed more time learning to write it. He didn't want his son to be at any more disadvantage than he naturally would be—being a child from another world.

Since it would be a two-year duty tour, he could request permission for Karlson to be enrolled in the Academy as planned, but be stationed aboard the *Seeker*, and to receive all the Junior Cadet instructional materials to be studied while onboard. The opportunity to learn while on a starship was unique. No other Junior Cadet—or even a full Cadet—had ever had this experience, since the students only went to space in the latter part of their Senior Cadet years.

After getting permission from the High Commander, who was also staying with the ship, Karl communicated with the Supreme Commander in charge of the Academy, and finally obtained his approval. Karlson was very happy at the idea of being on the ship for another two years, as he secretly had some doubts as to how he would fit in on a strange new world where all the kids his age would be taller than he was.

About one quarter of the crew decided to continue, and the rest prepared to go home. A cargo transport was dispatched to meet them with replacement crewmembers and enough supplies to last them for the two-year voyage to their distant destination.

*

With good-byes said, and the new crew and supplies onboard, the *Seeker* departed on its new mission. The next day, after returning from dinner, Karlson was surprised to find several large boxes stacked in his quarters. They were all addressed to him! He eagerly opened them. Uniforms! Cadet uniforms—for both cool and warm weather environments. And groups of them were in various sizes. And boots—just like his dad's! He tried on the smallest uniform—and it fit perfectly. Next came the boots. Most were too big, but he found a pair that was just right. He had enjoyed wearing an officer's uniform like his dad, but he wasn't really an officer yet, and didn't want anyone to think him silly by wearing one. But now, he was a Junior Cadet! A real Junior Cadet of the Academy!

He went to his father's quarters next to his. "Dad! Look!" He slowly made a full turn, showing his dad the new uniform.

"You look sharp!" Karl exclaimed, smiling broadly.

"This is great! I am a real Cadet!"

"You are a real *Junior* Cadet," Karl corrected. "After two years you will be promoted to full Cadet. And uniforms are not all that I ordered for you. You also have pressure suits and air-suits that should actually fit you properly; those were delivered to 'Pressure Suit Storage.'"

Since their quarters had limited storage space, Karlson put his new clothes into the closet, and Karl helped him pack up his "officer uniforms" plus all the cadet uniforms and boots that were still too big. He resealed the boxes and wrote a delivery note on each for storage in Ship's Services.

*

Karlson was officially back in school ... Academy Junior Cadet school, to be exact. One of the new crewmembers was Junior Airman Trace. He was barely out of the Academy himself, and the youngest crewmember—other than Karlson—so the High Commander assigned him to be Karlson's tutor. Trace was delighted, since he knew that being the most junior officer on the ship, he would most likely get the least enjoyable assignments. So, it turned out to be great. As he was not much more than a kid himself, he and Karlson got along very well. It was like Karlson had a new buddy!

Because Trace was the only Junior Airman on the ship, the officers called him "Junior." And, because Karlson was a Junior Cadet, they sometimes now called him "Junior" as well. It might seem that it would cause problems, but it didn't. It was pretty obvious who the Junior *Airman* was and who the Junior *Cadet* was. But, between the two of them when they were alone, Karlson called his tutor "Trace," and Trace called his student "Kid."

*

As they covered the lessons, Karlson learned a lot. He learned about the types of ships:

128

1. The non-space worthy Flyer Class (small personal craft like he had learned to pilot) that came in several sizes.

2. The space worthy classes, of which there were two: the Transports—for short distances (mini-shuttle, shuttle, mid-transport, and full sized transport) and the Starship Class (Cargo and deep space *Explorer* Class).

He also learned to speak "ship talk" where you call a hallway a "passageway," the ceiling was called "the overhead," some doors were called "hatches," the floor was the "deck" (but he already knew that one), stairs were "ladders," beds were "bunks," and left was "port" and right was "starboard." (Trace gave him an easy way to remember port and starboard—"left" and "port" both had four letters whereas "right" and "starboard" had more than four letters.)

He learned the Ranks of Service; there were two—Crewmen and Officers.

Crewman started at 10th class, then progressed to 1st class. First class crewmen were especially respected by all, including the officers. They were sometimes called "First Crew" or simply "First" for short.

Officers started at the Academy level: Junior Cadet, Cadet, and Senior Cadet. When they graduated they became a Junior Airman, then Airman, then Senior Airman, Sub-Commander, Commander, High Commander, and finally Supreme Commander—if they made it that high. Also, a First Class Crewman can jump to the officer ranks by going through special classes and then entering as an Airman.

It was a little bit confusing, because even though Crewman is a rank class, everyone on the ship is part of the crew—including officers. And, if there were a count of everyone, they called it "number of souls onboard."

Trace encouraged Karlson to ask questions. One of his first was to ask why the lady Airman officers were called Air*men* ... because they were women, not men. Trace explained that it would be awkward to call them Airwomen, so it was decided that because all humans are considered *man*kind, including women and children, that the term "man" could be used for both.

Then he asked: Who was more in charge, the Captain of the ship or the High Commander? Trace explained that the Captain (who was also a High Commander) managed the things that related to the ship, and the High Commander managed the missions.

A question that made Trace laugh was why the ship looked so ugly, instead of sleek and pretty, like some in the movies. Trace explained that the ship was designed for use *only* in space, where it was actually built. Everything was functional. The great hull that rotated gave a maximum useful area that had normal gravity. In times past, the ships had big rotating wheels, like a bicycle wheel rotating on its axel (hub), but the area with gravity was mostly in the outer "tire" part. Our ship here uses the same principle, but the "tire" is really, really wide, and thick—thick all the way to the hub, so we can have multiple decks. It just made better sense, and who cares if the ship is ugly or not?

Karlson asked: Why not let the ship's main body spin slower and therefore produce less gravity, so everyone could run and jump easier to get from place to place? Trace explained that low gravity was not really good to be in for extended periods of time, because the body's muscles wouldn't have to work very hard to move a person around, and they would lose their strength. If you don't use it ... you lose it!

*

Thankfully, book studies weren't the only lessons. Some of the lessons were kind of boring, as school can be, but not always.

Once they went to the Dead Zone to practice safe moves in a zero-gravity environment. As they climbed the steps up through the decks, Trace told Karlson about his first experience in zero-grav at the Academy.

"I puked my guts out."

"No!"

"Yeah, the instructor warned us that we might get sick and if we felt it, *not* to continue, but I didn't want anyone to think I wasn't up to it. So, after only a minute in there, I hurled and hurled. Great big chunks of puke just floated around. When my stomach had finally turned inside out—that's what it felt like—I had to get the barf bags and capture each glob... and did it ever stink!"

"That's disgusting!" Karlson laughed.

"Yeah, kid, but I deserved it. I was the one who didn't follow instructions, so why should someone else have to clean up my mess?"

"I guess you're right," Karlson agreed. "I was lucky; zero-grav never affected me."

"Yeah, you were lucky. Most of us had to deal with it until we got used to it, which even I eventually did ... now it's kinda fun!"

So, they reviewed the safety protocols (which mostly were just about wearing the mag-belt, avoiding the openings, and not cracking your head into the walls), and then they just goofed off— doing crazy maneuvers like somersaults and flips.

*

One day Trace took Karlson to the Laser Range! Normally, weapons training didn't take place until the Senior Cadet level. But, every member of the crew (from the lowest crewman 10th class rank to the Captain and High Commander) took refresher courses at the laser range. So, Trace reasoned, why not the kid as well?

They had to wait until the range was clear before Trace would begin Karlson's first lesson. They reviewed the safety instructions: Never point a laser pistol or any weapon at anyone, or even in anyone's general direction. The weapon's safety latch was to remain in locked position until ready to shoot. When leaving for a possibly dangerous mission that required bringing a weapon, always check for a reading of "full" on the pistol's charge. And when on that dangerous mission, keep your finger OFF the trigger—keep it straight along the outside of the trigger opening, until ready to fire.

Then Trace gave Karlson a fully loaded weapon ... Now, let's be real here. It wasn't an *actual* laser pistol—it was a training pistol, which operated, weighed, and looked (except for a colored band around the muzzle) just the same as a real one, but shot a simple light beam instead of a seriously deadly laser beam.

Then the fun began. They practiced hitting stationary targets. When the light beam struck the target, it left a colored mark that corresponded with the colored band on the laser pistol that shot it. Trace showed him how to aim properly and squeeze the trigger. He was a pretty good shot, and Karlson learned quickly from him. Each training pistol left a different colored mark, so it soon became a game! It was sort of like playing darts, except that you didn't have to go pick them out of the board so you could play more. After several lessons, they graduated to moving targets. That was much harder. But also more fun!

When they were alone in the range, they upped the game. Because the laser range was on deck B, the gravity there was a bit less than the normal gravity on deck A. So ... they were able to leap about easier, do rolls and all kinds of moves, then come up shooting at the moving targets. Sometimes they even managed to hit one! Trace was better at it than Karlson, but they each gave the other a good challenge.

On his off-duty time, Karl took the boy to the range too. Being an expert marksman himself, he was more than qualified to further instruct his son. They didn't flip and roll around, but Karlson and his dad always had a great time together.

Chapter 16

A Walk on the Wild Side

One morning, Karl said there would be no school lessons for that day, and explained why. He, plus a group of others, had to check the hull of the ship for any problems. It was a continual and tedious task, with groups taking turns checking sections of the massive hull. It was such a huge job, that most everyone onboard had to take a turn at it.

"So ... want to take a walk with me on the 'wild side'?" Karl asked.

"The 'what' side?" Karlson questioned.

Karl laughed. "I don't know where the term got started, but that's what we call it when we go out and walk the outer hull ... in space."

"Really? I can go with you into outer space?"

"Yes, everyone needs to know how to handle themselves in that environment ... it's a safety requirement. And, it will give you a chance to try out your suit—the one that actually fits you."

"My space suit?"

"No, your *pressure* suit ... although it actually *is* a space suit, but it can be used in other situations, like where there is low pressure. Do you understand 'pressure'?"

"Uh, I'm not sure. I understand gravity and mass ... is it like that?"

"No, not really. In our use here, pressure is the force that an atmosphere (the air) presses against you. Do you remember what it felt like on a dreary rainy day back on your home planet, and how you felt on a bright sunny day?"

"Yes, sir, I felt unhappy and wet on the rainy days, but on the sunny days I felt good, because we could hunt for food."

"Well, putting aside the things you *did* on those days, the atmospheric air pressure is *lower* on rainy days and *higher* on sunny days. Your body has pressure within it, so it reacts with the pressure changes in the weather. Our ship is pressurized at a certain point for our comfort. Do you know what it would be like to be in a very *highly* pressurized place?"

Karlson shook his head.

"Because your body would be at a lower pressure, the high pressure would push upon you—squeezing you ... crushing you until your bones would break, and you would be crushed to death."

Karlson grimaced at the idea.

"Now, what would happen to you in an *un*pressurized place, like outer space, where there is no atmosphere at all?"

"I'm afraid to ask," he said.

Karl laughed. "It's horrible there too. Your body's pressure would push your flesh outward into the lack of pressure—and you would ... explode."

"Like a bomb?"

"No, not like a bomb. Maybe 'explode' is the wrong term. Your body fluids would bubble, like boil but without heat, and the body tissues would expand. You would end up more like a big bubbly gooey mess. So, you see, we take pressure *very* seriously. That's why we always have a pressure suit along when we go anywhere."

Karlson thought for a moment. "When we were back on my planet, did we have pressure suits along when we took the transport to see the High Commander?"

"You got me there, son. No, we didn't. That's the only case where we don't bring our personal suits, when we take simple trips to and from a planet base. But ... the transports *do* always have enough pressure suits stored in cargo—one for every seat. It's still a safety requirement. We take the preservation of life very seriously."

*

Karl and Karlson arrived at "Pressure Suit Storage" where Crewman Jenner gave Karlson a new pressure suit that Karl had ordered—one that would fit him perfectly! Jenner had already put the boy's name on it. They both laughed at remembering how ridiculous he had looked in that other full-sized suit they had tried to adjust down for him.

Both Crewman Jenner and his dad helped him into the suit, attached his utility belt, and re-educated him in the use of the controls. The "pack" (which they called the air/pressure unit located on the back of the suit) was a bit heavy, but otherwise the suit was fine—even the gloves fit. Carrying the helmet, they thanked Crewman Jenner, and left for the nearby "Active Astronaut" locker room to get Karl's suit.

It was a little crowded in the astronaut room as about twelve other people were suiting up, including Karl. One by one they left, all carrying their helmets, for stairs that led up through all the decks to deck F, where a small airlock was located.

Now that Karlson was officially an Academy Junior Cadet, Karl changed the way they interacted. When in a "teaching" situation, he addressed his son as "Junior" or "Junior Cadet," and Karlson addressed his dad as "Commander" or "Sir."

Noticing Karlson's struggle to climb the steps with the heavy pack on his suit back, he questioned, "Junior Cadet, what happens to our weight as we approach Deck B, then C and so on?"

"Sir, our weight will become less and less."

"Correct! Why?"

"Because the closer we get to the zero-hub, the less centrifugal force is exerted upon us."

"Correct again!" As they passed deck B, the Commander asked smiling, "Are you feeling the lesser gravity now?"

"Yes, sir, the steps are getting easier."

"Junior, we are going to an airlock close to the hub ... what would happen to us if we exited the ship at a place on the outer hull at a *maximum* distance from zero-hub?"

Karlson thought a moment before answering. "At a maximum distance from zero-hub, like deck A, the centrifugal force caused by the rotation of the ship would throw us outward, which is what we want because it gives us an artificial gravity. But, if we left the ship there, as soon as we opened the airlock hatch, we would be thrown out into space! And drift away forever and ever ... if we didn't have our jets."

"Excellent, Junior, so why do we exit the ship close to zero-hub, on the front—near the array?"

"Because, sir, the centrifugal force is much less there, and when we go out and let go, we won't be thrown out very much."

"Very good." Karl laughed, "Now what is our procedure *before* we enter the airlock and before we exit it?"

"We double check our suits for a 'full' reading. We put our helmets on and hear the click to know that it's secure. Then we turn on our pressure and temperature controls. If everything is 'green lights,' we go in and cycle the airlock, and then we go out."

"You left out one important step, Junior Cadet, remember the 'being thrown out and drift away forever' part? What do we do before the outer hatch of the airlock opens to space?"

"Oh, we always secure our tether straps to the ship!"

"Yes! Safety is everything."

They arrived at an airlock off the very low-gravity deck F. Everyone followed procedure, locking their helmets and engaging internal pressure which made their suits puff up. Karlson could only hear his breathing in the silence inside his secured helmet, and maybe his own heartbeat (but that was probably only his imagination).

Half of the group entered the airlock—it wasn't quite big enough for them all to fit. The inner hatch door closed. Karlson watched the readouts showing the air being pumped out of the airlock. The outer hatch opened and the first group exited out to space from the airlock. After a few moments, the outer hatch door closed and the airlock recycled, pumping air back into the small room, and then the inner hatch door opened for the remaining group.

They went in and immediately secured their tether straps to the bar just inside the outer hatch door, plus Karl snapped a second tether line from his belt to Karlson's ... just in case. The inner hatch door closed behind them and the air was pumped out. Then the outer hatch opened to space.

Each man held tightly onto the hand-hold bar next to the outer hatch and deftly flipped himself out, then unhooked his tether from the inner tether bar and reattached it to the outer tether bar. They all were out, and then Karl was out, floating among the others.

Karlson heard the radio break the silence in his helmet, "Your turn, Junior."

Karlson did exactly as his father had done. He held the bar and flipped himself out of the hatch. Still holding the hand-hold bar, he unhooked his tether from the inside tether bar and attached it to the outer bar. He turned to the others ... he was out in the vast darkness of space ... and falling!

Forgetting protocol in his panic, he yelled, "Dad! I'm falling!"

"No!" Karl said firmly, "Look at me! You are NOT falling! It's an illusion!" Karl grabbed the boy and turned him so that his feet aimed at the hull. "Now, look at the ship. That is your new 'ground.' Turn on your mag-boots."

Controlling his panic, Karlson said breathlessly, "Yes, sir," and flipped the magnetic boot switch on his belt. His feet clicked onto the hull and stayed firmly there.

"You OK now, Junior?"

"Y-Yes, sir." Karlson took a deep breath, "Sorry, sir."

"It's my fault, I should have warned you. The illusion of falling bothers some people at first, until they get used to it."

The others waited patiently, floating about, still tethered to the ship.

Karl, being team leader, said, "Everyone ready?"

"Yes, sir ... Yes, Commander ..." the voices came over the radio in Karlson's helmet.

"Forgive me, fellas, while I explain things to our young trainee here."

"Not a problem, Commander," a voice said.

"Yes, it might make this less boring, since we can't play any music," came another voice.

"Someone could sing ..."

"But not you, First, you sound like a ..."

Then the Captain's voice came on, "Knock off the excess chatter; the sooner you get the job done, the better."

"Yes, sir, Captain!" all voices said in unison.

"Proceed with your lesson, Commander."

"Thank you, Captain," Karl replied.

One by one the white suited figures detached their tethers and floated a short distance from the ship. Then wisps of vapor shot out of their directional jets, pushing them along their way to their designated search area.

Karlson watched with fascination, wondering why they had released their safety tethers, but was afraid to ask a possibly stupid question, knowing that the Captain was listening in.

Karl watched his son, anticipating his confusion. "Junior Cadet, are you wondering why they detached their safety tethers?"

"Yes, sir, I am."

"In this case, they have to. We are each going to search a portion of the hull, looking for any dings from space debris, or anything unusual. When we get to our search point, we will reattach the tether to an imbedded tether bar—there are thousands all over the hull—and engage our mag-boots so we can walk the hull on our portion of the search grid. Do you know why we use our jets rather than walk with our mag-boots to the search areas?"

"I think so, sir." Karlson said, remembering his long trips exploring the ship. "Is it because it would take hours to walk there if your search area was way off down the hull?"

"It certainly would. Are you ready to release your mag-boots? Can you overcome the feeling of falling?"

"I think so, sir." Karlson took a deep breath. "I do just fine with zero-gravity; I don't know why I thought I was falling."

"It's because the zero-gravity chamber has walls ... outer space does not. Just focus on the hull, and you should be fine. Ready?"

"Ready," Karlson said as he turned off the magnetic boots. He immediately began floating. "I'm OK."

"Good, ready to learn how to fly?"

"Fly?"

"Yes, using your jets. Go ahead and unhook your tether and retract it. Then release your jet control bar."

Karlson detached his tether line from the ship and pushed the retract button. The tether rewound back to his belt. Then he reached back and pushed the button that released the arm rest with the jet controls on it. It swung around, locked into place, and he put his hand on the control lever. Crewman Jenner had previously explained how it worked, so he was ready.

"We are attached, so where you go, I go too. Remember, short bursts on the jets. There is no friction or atmosphere in space, so you will move and continue moving, until you use another jet burst ... or bump into something. Now, give a short burst forward."

He did, and off they went! It wasn't fast, but that was just fine with Karlson. He was tilting a bit crooked, so Karl said, "Adjust your position in relation to the hull. You want the hull 'down' beneath your feet. This will help your equilibrium as well as your direction."

Karlson gave a short burst and moved just a little, tilting back some toward a level position in regard to the ship's hull.

"Give another *very* short burst to stop your tilt turn," said his father's voice.

He gave a tiny blast of his jet for the opposite direction, stopping his turn so that he was now going fairly straight along the hull.

"Look ahead. Do you see the suit? He is going to make the edge turn very soon. There! See? He went around the edge. We left the ship on the front, next to zero-hub. We need to go to the outer edge of the front—farthest from the hub—and then turn onto the long side of the hull."

Yes, Karlson thought, we are at the end of the "hotdog bun," next to the array (which is the hotdog sticking out of the bun). We need to go from the front of the bun to the long side of the bun. He was glad his dad didn't mention over the radio about his "hotdog" comparison to the starship, because he knew the crew would kid him about it forever—especially Trace!

It seemed like Karlson was traveling forward alone, because he couldn't see his father trailing along behind, attached to him with the tether strap. He was passing a giant hatch door with a huge number on it. "Commander, what are these big doors for?"

"Those are hangar doors. Look above and below. Those round openings are docking ports. Do you remember when we docked in the transport? The docking ports and hangar bays alternate all around the end here at the front of the ship. On the rear of the ship are the big cargo bays—we can only use them when the star-drive engines are in neutral. Most of the docking ports and hangar bays here on the front—they exit onto deck A, so that passengers won't have any disruption of gravity. When a transport docks nose first into a docking port, it essentially becomes an appendage on the hull that is always rotating, as you know. It's a tricky maneuver to match the rotating hull, that's why transport pilots use 'computer-assist' in the docking procedure."

Karlson thought of his "hotdog in a fat bun" starship ... a docked transport would look like a fly sitting on the front end of the bun! He smiled at his mental picture.

"Come to a stop," Karl's voice said. The boy gave the lever a quick movement back, making a short forward jet blast, slowing him enough for Karl to float up next to him. Because Karlson's jet stopped only Karlson, not Karl, his dad kept moving forward with his continued momentum. Karl grabbed the boy, slowing himself down.

"Well done, Junior. Ready for your solo? I'm detaching my tether strap from you and we're going to continue together down the long side of the hull."

By then, they both had floated just a little beyond the front end of the ship. Karl pointed to the direction they would be going. Karlson drew in a quick breath. "Wow!" he blurted out, "I know the ship is big, but this is *really* big!" And it was. It seemed like before them were miles and miles of metal. Karlson could hear muffled laughter on the radio.

"It *is* big, and our search grid section is way down there, so let's go!"

Together, each on his own jet power, they headed off down the hull. "Should we go faster?" Karlson asked.

Again he heard some stifled laughter over the radio.

"No, Junior, we don't need to. We'll be there soon enough. We always use the least amount of jet that we need. Always conserve your energy, especially out here. Safety first, as always."

Karl checked the grid map attached to his sleeve. "Here we are. Get as close to the hull as you can ... gently ... and come to a stop. Now, engage your mag-boots. Retract your jet controls and attach your tether here."

Karlson followed the instructions. He pulled the lever back and the reverse jets fired, slowing him. He was still going too fast so he gave another short blast of jet. He turned on his mag-boots and gently touched the metal hull. Click went his boots, and his feet stuck to the hull. He pushed the button to retract his jet controls. Then he carefully walked over and hooked his tether onto an imbedded hull bracket, next to his father's. Now they both were ready.

"We are looking for anything that isn't right ... like dings—small indentations that a bit of space debris might make if it struck the hull hard enough."

"Isn't the hull real thick?"

"Yes, it is, but something traveling extremely fast, even something tiny, might penetrate the hull. That rarely happens, but if it did, it's serious. We would lose both our breathing air and our pressure. Do you remember what we discussed about pressure?"

"Yes, sir, I do."

"The airtight hatches within the ship would close automatically to control the problem, but it is still quite dangerous. When we walk the hull, we're looking for anything that is less than that kind of a catastrophic hit, but could be a *potential* problem. Again, safety first ... this ship is our only home out here!"

Karlson glanced upward, and realized that the stars were gone! "Dad, uh, Commander, what happened to the stars? They're gone!"

Karl chuckled, "They are still there, I assure you. In space, there's no atmosphere, and that affects the light from the stars. Also, any other light around will 'wash out' the dim light of the stars. Since our ship has bright lights out here, we can't see the stars."

Karlson thought for a moment, "But sir, we can see them from the viewports in the ship while we're in space."

Karl answered, "Yes, that's because our viewports have been ... designed so that the stars are visible to us. The same is true for the transports and shuttles; you can see the stars from those viewports as well. But, individual helmets are just made of strong transparent material, with no special treatment, so we don't usually see the stars when we're in our suits."

"Oh," was all Karlson could say. He liked seeing the stars.

Just then a voice said, "Found something! It's a small dimple, not deep, but deep enough. Marking it now ... Grid 435 ... Section C ... coordinates D by 45."

Then the Captain's voice came on, "Receiving marker transmission."

Karl explained. "When we find something, we call in the coordinates and place a radio marker on it—one of these (he pointed to a small lumpy bag attached to his belt)—which sends a signal that we can pick up *inside* the hull, to find the exact location of the problem ... so we can see if we can detect it on the inside as well as outside. Anything we can see on the inside is serious—because it has weakened the hull. Don't worry, we send a maintenance crew to evaluate and fix it."

About an hour and a half into their scheduled two-hour walk, and finding nothing, something suddenly popped on the hull between them.

Even before Karl could call out a warning, the Captain's voice yelled in all their ears, "Incoming! Incoming!"

Karl exclaimed to his son, "Turn off your mag-boots! Retract the tether!"

"What's ..." Karlson began.

"Not now, just do what I say!" his dad interrupted.

They each released their boots and engaged their automatic tether retract, and were pulled quickly to the tether bracket on the hull. Karl reattached his second tether to the boy's belt. "Unhook your tether to the ship! Do NOT engage your jets—I'm driving!"

They each unhooked their tether straps from the hull, and Karl immediately engaged his jet controls. He fired his forward jets and swiftly flew down the long stretch of hull with Karlson being pulled behind him like a tail ... and going faster and faster! Karl didn't even slow down at the turn—he expertly managed his jets as he careened around from the long side to the front of the ship, swinging Karlson way out and around behind him. If it weren't just a bit scary, it would have been great fun! Then Karl slowed, allowing Karlson to pass him, and he used his reverse jets to slow them both more and more until they were stopped at the airlock. Several members of their team were already there, entering the airlock's open hatch. Karl unhooked his tether from the boy's belt and shoved him in with them, while he remained outside waiting for the rest of his team. The airlock outer hatch closed. As quickly as it could cycle, it was open again, and the rest of the team entered the safety of the ship.

"Commander!" came the anxious Captain's voice over the radio.

"All accounted for, sir ... what happened?" Karl replied.

"Heavy dust, Commander, we didn't detect it until it was right up on us. Stand down. We won't send out any teams until tomorrow. We should be clear of the dust by then. Captain out."

They all removed their helmets and began the trip back down to deck A. "Dad, what happened?" Karlson whispered as they walked down the steps.

"We were hit with a cloud of space dust ... very tiny particles of meteor rock. It usually doesn't hurt the ship, but the tiny pieces can *easily* puncture a pressure suit ... that's why we had to get out of there immediately. We will have to leave our suits with Crewman Jenner to be tested for any possible damage. Sometimes there can be a tiny puncture tear, which we might not notice at first, but could be a huge problem the next trip out."

Karlson thought about what had just happened. No one really seemed upset except for the Captain. Any one of the hull walkers could have been killed at any moment, but no one said anything about it as they chatted lightly with each other while going down the steps. He guessed that they were either very brave or just used to the dangers of space ... probably both.

* * *

146

It was evening, and Karlson had finished his math lesson homework. He walked to his father's quarters and in through the open doorway. His dad was just signing off on the video-com ... from an apparent conversation with that lady, Alana!

"Dad, was that Senior Airman Alana?"

"Yes," Karl said, slightly embarrassed. "We talk occasionally."

"*I* didn't know that," the boy said.

"Well, it's not a *secret*; I just ... must not have mentioned it before," Karl said with a guilty laugh.

"You *like* her, don't you?" The boy just stood there grinning. "You *like* her!"

"Of course I like her, everyone likes her, don't you like her?"

"Sure, but you *like* her!" Karlson teased. "You LIKE her!"

Karl picked up a pillow and tossed it at the boy, laughing. "Go on, monster!"

Karlson deftly caught the pillow and tossed it back. He left still taunting, "You like her! You like her!"

"You just wait, son, your turn will come!" he heard his father call after him, still laughing. "I promise!"

Chapter 17

Deadly Marble

The Captain, Karl, Trace, and Karlson were the last people in the dining room to leave, as they were still enjoying their after-dinner conversation, when the alarms went off.

"HULL BREACH" flashed the large letters on the info screens, alternating with "A 145, A 146."

Everyone jumped up from the table, knocking their chairs backward, and took off running toward compartments A 145 and A 146. Karlson tried to keep up as best he could.

As the Captain ran, he yelled into his uniform radio microphone, "Everyone out?"

"No! Three trapped!" came the immediate response.

"Control, max pressure to 145 and 146!"

"Already on it, Captain!"

"Suits to breach!" the Captain yelled again into the radio.

"On their way, Captain!" came another voice.

When they arrived at compartment 144, which was next to 145, several crewmen were quickly putting on pressure suits that had just been carried there by breathlessly panting (half collapsed to their knees) crewmembers from "Pressure Suit Storage." The Captain looked through the small round window in the airtight hatch door that had automatically slid closed between 144 and 145.

"One person down in 145! The other two must be in 146! Why is the hatch in there still open?"

"Don't know, Captain, it appears to be stuck!"

The crewmember lying on the deck in 145 began shaking all over. "He's convulsing!"

Every second counted. The people trapped unconscious in the two compartments were suffering from lack of air and pressure. By raising the airflow to maximum into those two rooms, the Captain hoped to compensate for some of the oxygen and air pressure being lost into outer space through the hull breach—the hole that had been punched into the ship.

"We're going to use this compartment as an airlock! Let's go!" the Captain shouted.

Everyone not in a pressure suit quickly exited out of compartment 144 and into the passageway. They used the "manual override" to slide closed the airtight hatch door between them and 144. (All automatic airtight hatch doors normally remain hidden between the walls at most every doorway within the ship—until they are needed.)

As soon as the sliding hatch door closed completely, one of the five pressure-suited crewmen pushed the manual override button to 145, and the airtight hatch door to that room began to open. *Swoosh* went the air (at normal pressure in 144) into the lower and constantly decreasing pressure in 145 and 146. Two pressure-suited crewmen unceremoniously grabbed the gasping writhing man from the deck of 145 and carried/dragged him into 144. After barely clearing the doorway, they pushed the close button and the airtight hatch door slid closed behind them. The air pressure in 144 quickly rose to normal, and they opened the airtight hatch door to the waiting medical team in the passageway.

Of the three pressure-suited men left in 145, one began searching for the hole in the hull, from which they could barely hear a squealing/hissing sound as the air rushed out into the vacuum of space. The other two men tried to open the stuck hatch door between 145 and 146. They could hear the whining of the straining motor—the automatic door was still tying to close! They pushed the override button, but nothing happened.

They tried to squeeze through the partial opening but only their helmets cleared—their suits didn't because of their large bodies plus the pack on the back. They could see the two people on the deck inside, unconscious, and very much in trouble.

"Need to cut the cables to the door motor!" The Captain called over the radio.

"The access panel is in there! Can't get through!" exclaimed the two men. "We're too big!"

"What about the kid?" Trace blurted out.

The words were barely out of his mouth before Karl was lifting Karlson into a spare suit. They madly tightened the leg and arm straps to make the suit as small as possible. They half carried him into 144 while they secured his helmet. They flipped his pressure on, and his suit filled and puffed out. Suit functions were all green lights. They handed him a tool bag which he gripped between his too large gloves. Then they were gone, the airtight hatch slid closed, and he was alone in 144. He turned toward the already opening hatch to 145. Swoosh went the air! One of the men took the tool bag and rushed him to the malfunctioning door, explaining what to do—get in there and open a maintenance panel and then cut the red wire.

Karlson stuck his helmeted head through the partially open hatch door. The two men squished the fabric of his suit tight around him, making him small enough to clear both himself plus his back pack. Through the hatch he went! He saw the two people

150

on the deck—they were gasping for air, writhing and shaking violently. Their faces and bodies were swollen, their eyes bulged out from their eye sockets and blood was coming from their noses ... they barely looked human. He immediately turned from them to the bubble-helmeted head and white-suited arm that poked through the crack of the malfunctioning hatch door.

"Here, take this and open the panel next to the door!" The crewman held out a power screwdriver that was already turned on. Karlson's fingers barely entered the finger holes of his gloves—which made them more like big mittens than actual gloves—so he held it between both his hands.

"Open the panel!"

He could barely see over the bottom of the helmet, because the suit was so big, as he put the turning driver blade into a screw. One, then the other he quickly unscrewed, letting them fall to the deck. Then the panel cover dropped to the deck.

"Here! Cut the red wire! Or cut them all if you don't see it!" The crewman's thick white-suited arm stretched out toward him with a large cutter held in his glove. "Hurry!"

Karlson dropped the power driver and grabbed the cutter. He could see the red wire but it was buried among several others. So, he opened the cutter jaw-blades wide, shoved it into the whole mess of wires, and pushed the handles together with all his strength, cutting all the wires at once. The whine of the airtight door motor ceased. The two men, plus the third man that had unsuccessfully searched for the hole, shoved and slid the disabled door back into the wall. Ignoring Karlson, they grabbed the two dying people and dragged them as fast as they could through the now fully open hatchway, through 145, and into 144. Karlson grabbed and lifted a dangling twitching leg and tried to help as best he could. As soon as the airtight hatch door closed behind them all, the pressure quickly equalized and the hatch door opened in front of them. The two rescued people were heaved up and dumped onto the waiting gurneys. The two medical teams turned and raced toward Medical, pushing the gurneys— strapping their thrashing patients in as they ran.

"Seal it!" the Captain ordered. The control room sealed compartments 145 and 146, cutting the airflow being pumped in, which was now being wasted as it hissed out into outer space.

As the team removed their suits, all the Captain said to the boy was, "Well done, Junior."

Karlson felt very pleased. No one had asked him if he would go, they just assumed that he would. He wasn't treated special or less than special. He was part of the team ... part of the crew, and that was all that mattered.

About an hour later, the notice came over the entire ship's intercom: All three of the rescued people were expected to fully recover.

It ended up as a good day.

*

Unknown to anyone else, the Captain sent out two transmission memos. The first was to Central Command suggesting that in future starship designs, *all* compartments should have at least two exits, and he illustrated his reasoning by explaining what had happened. The second memo went to the Supreme Commander at the Academy. In it he suggested that, in the near future, they may wish to consider allowing a Junior Cadet to serve aboard a starship where at least one parent was already serving. He explained how Karlson, being small, had been such an asset in the repair of the forward array, and especially how he had been instrumental in saving the lives of two crewmen.

When the Supreme Commander at the Academy received the memo, he was very pleased to know that his Junior Cadet was proving to be a valuable asset to the crew, and included the memo in Karlson's permanent record.

*

A couple of days later, a hull maintenance crewman found Karlson and said, "Captain said to give this to you. It's the larger meteor that hit and penetrated the hull. There were actually two of them, but one disintegrated. It was a freak thing, the way one imbedded into the airtight door track—keeping it from closing, and one of the fragments from the other took out the override control to that door. Really freaky."

He deposited a small clear plastic bag into Karlson's hand. Inside was a black rock, about the size of a marble.

Chapter 18

The Man with the Black Eye-patch

Commander Karl had just left to resume his daily duties. Lunch was over, but Trace and Karlson were still there eating a second helping of ice cream. A man with a black patch over his eye walked over to their table.

"Hello, Junior Cadet Karlson."

"Uh, hello sir," Karlson answered quizzically.

"You don't remember me, do you?" he asked the boy.

Karlson glanced from the man to Trace and back to the man again. "No, sir, I..."

"Junior Cadet Karlson, I'm Sub-Commander Palants." He held out his hand to the boy. Karlson hopped off his chair, stood and shook his hand.

Karlson introduced Trace, "Sir, this is Junior Airman Trace."

Trace stood and shook the Sub-Commander's hand. "Please join us, sir," Trace offered, and they all sat down.

"You saved my life, young man—that's what I was told," Sub-Commander Palants began. "I was in compartment 146 with two others. All I remember is that the next compartment was hit and losing air, but the automatic airtight door would not close all the way to seal and protect our compartment. Override didn't work, so since the hatch door was still partially open, we tried to push it open more so we could get into that next compartment, go through it, and get out through the next one. Only one of us managed to squeeze through the hatch. That's all I remember until I woke up in Medical."

"Oh, yes, sir, but it wasn't just me, a bunch of us got you all out."

"I realize that, but if you had not been there, and been able to squeeze through that damaged hatch and kill the power, the two of us trapped in there would have died for sure ... in fact, we were halfway there ... to death, I mean. We must have looked just horrible—quite a sight!"

Remembering their gasps for air, blood coming out of their noses, their bulging eyes, and their inhuman looking swollen bodies convulsing wildly, he nodded. "Yes, sir, I'm glad we were able to get the job done in time."

"Me too. I'm on light duty right now, but I am a transport pilot. Have you ever been in the cockpit of a transport before?"

"No, sir."

"Would you like to check it out?"

"Yes, sir, I really would!" Karlson answered eagerly.

"I will clear it with the Captain," Sub-Commander Palants said, rising from his chair. "And I'll contact you soon."

They all stood again, shook hands, and the man with the black eye-patch left.

*

True to his word, Sub-Commander Palants obtained permission from the Captain, spoke to Commander Karl, and arranged for Karlson to visit the hangar deck, Bay 4. When Karlson arrived at the agreed on time, Sub-Commander Palants was already there waiting for him.

"Thank you, sir, for giving me this opportunity," Karlson said politely.

"Glad to do it, Junior Cadet," he smiled. "Let's get aboard."

They climbed the ramp and entered the big elongated egg-shaped transport. They passed through the plush passenger section and then climbed several steps to the cockpit. There were two pilot seats and two fold-up "jump seats"—for extra cockpit seating. Sub-Commander Palants showed Karlson the controls, and explained how the transport ship operated. It was much more complicated than a flyer. When they were done, the Sub-Commander said, "Ready to take a shuttle out?"

"Sir?"

"Yes, I have permission, even with my bum eye, to take you out and give you a piloting lesson. How would you like that?"

"Oh, yes, sir, I would like that *very* much," Karlson nodded and grinned excitedly.

"OK then, let's go!"

They left Bay 4 and walked to the much smaller Bay 8, where a mini-shuttle sat. They climbed the two steps on the landing strut and entered the opening. Palants turned to close and secure the airtight hatch, and then they went to the front pilot seats. "You take the co-pilot seat," he said to the boy.

Karlson sat in it, but because it was sized for an adult Star Man, it was far too big. "Let's take care of that." Palants unsnapped the cushions off the two jump seats that were on this craft as well as the larger transport, and put them behind the boy. "Good?"

"Yes, sir, perfect!" Then Karlson remembered, "Sir, aren't we supposed to get our pressure suits? Doesn't everyone have to bring their suit along on any trips into space?"

"*Very* good, Junior! I'm impressed that you know that. Yes, we *do* have to bring our pressure suits aboard, and there they are." He pointed back into the craft. "I brought them here myself."

Karlson looked where the Sub-Commander was pointing, and there they were ... two bright white suits hanging in the rear, one large and one small.

Palants called the control room of the starship, "Hangar Control, Sub-Commander Palants in Shuttle 8, requesting permission to disembark from Bay 8, duration for less than an hour."

A voice on the radio said, "Shuttle 8, permission granted."

"Cycling," Palants said.

Immediately the alarms went off in Bay 8. After a few moments, the hangar hatch door behind them slowly lowered. Then the air was pumped out, and the big space doors opened in front of their small craft. Palants explained each maneuver as he executed it. The shuttle rose off the hangar deck smoothly and he flipped on the switch for the craft's artificial gravity. Slowly they moved forward and passed between the open space doors. "We exit at the front of the ship—do you know why?"

"Yes, sir, my dad explained how all the hangar bay doors are like in a ring around the front of the ship, so that the gravity caused by the rotation of the ship's main hull will be the same in the docking bays, so we can more safely leave and enter the ship."

"Correct. Have you ever seen these docks from the outside before?"

"Yes, sir, when my dad and I went to the 'wild side.'"

"You've walked the hull?" Palants was surprised.

"Yes, sir, until we were hit with space dust, then we had to get back in fast."

"You were in *that*?"

"Yes, sir, but I wasn't scared."

"I would have been!" he laughed. "Now, we are turning ... see the square bay we just came out of? Look above it ... see a round docking port? Those are for big transports to soft dock into, when we go to and from a planet frequently. You've ridden on a transport before, haven't you?"

"Yes, sir ... please don't tell anyone, but I think it looks like a big long egg!"

Palants laughed, "I guess it really does. The round front end of the "egg" goes into the round docking port, locks on, and then we transfer passengers through the front exit. When we're done, we undock and go back to the planet. It saves more energy than cycling the hangar airlocks. But when we're on a voyage, like now, we keep the transports in the hangars."

"Ready to go for a ride? Take the controls, and turn the shuttle like you just saw me do."

Karlson did as he was told, and carefully turned the small craft so that it pointed out to open space. "Now, gently push the throttle lever forward, just a little."

He did, and they were off!

"See this readout? It shows our distance from the ship, which is our reference point 'zero.' Let's go out further ... push it!"

Karlson pushed the throttle forward, and their speed increased.

"This readout shows our speed, in relation to the starship. You see, even if we were at a dead stop, we would still be hurtling through space because the universe is expanding. You know that a moon revolves around its planet, and the planet then revolves around its sun—which is a star. But did you know that all solar systems are revolving about the central mass of our galaxy? And our galaxy is also traveling very fast through space? So, you see, speed is relative. In our case, we use a measured distance per second for our speed. Do you know what the speed of light is?"

"Yes, sir, it is approximately 186,000 miles per second."

"Do you know what a light-*year* is?"

"Yes, sir, it is the *distance* that light can travel in a vacuum in a period of one standard solar year, which works out to be almost 6 trillion miles."

"Excellent, you must be a good student."

"I try, and my instructor, Junior Airman Trace, thinks I'm doing OK."

"Good, let's do a 180 degree turn ... you know what that is, right?"

"Yes, sir, it's basically a turn around where we face the direction we just came from."

"But we are in space ... does that make a difference?" Palants asked.

Karlson thought a moment. "If we are considering a two dimensional travel surface—like a road on the ground where direction is basically forward and back, but no up or down, then no. But in space, there are all directions, including up or down and all around, so that might be confusing ... at least it confuses me."

"Well, you're not alone. When we say 'make a 180,' we are referencing a direction relative to our ship or our departure point. It's a habit, because it really *isn't* a proper term to use here in space ... so, make your turn and let's head back to the ship."

Karlson made the turn, and they headed back. As they approached the starship, Karlson reduced speed and came to a stop, as he was instructed. Before them was a closed hangar bay door with a great big number 8 on it.

"You have done very well. Your movements are smooth and steady ..." Sub-Commander Palants hesitated, "Do you think you can land in the shuttle bay?"

"I ... I think so sir, I can land a flyer ..."

"This is a bit different. Call the ship. You say 'Hangar Control, Shuttle 8 requesting permission to re-enter Bay 8,' and then we wait for permission and for the space doors to fully open."

Karlson tapped the microphone on and said in his best non-nervous voice, "Hangar Control, Shuttle 8 requesting permission to re-enter Bay 8."

There was a moment of silence, and then a voice from the ship answered, "Shuttle 8, permission granted to re-enter and land in Bay 8."

Sub-Commander Palants chuckled, "I guess they weren't expecting a boy's voice!"

A few minutes passed while the hangar airlock cycled. Karlson was uneasy about the landing. The shuttle was quite a bit larger than a flyer, and this landing area was inside the ship, not in a field ... and the hangar was small—very small!

"Now, if I say 'my controls' you let go of everything *instantly*, and I will take over, got it?"

"Yes, sir," Karlson gulped.

"We use these other controls for docking ... see? This screen indicates our shuttle in relation to the opening. Keep the image of the shuttle squarely in and equally distant from all sides ... the numbers on the sides of the image show your distance from the hatch opening and the walls of the interior. If you get too close to any side, the green distance numbers will turn red. If you get *way* too close, an alarm will sound. The number in the center of the screen is the distance marker that centers us inside the hangar bay—front to back. It will count down to zero as you enter. When it's at zero, cut your forward momentum to neutral. Don't look out the front viewport, just watch the screen, and don't panic. When the readout is at zero, I'll tell you what to do next."

Karlson's eyes were big as saucers. This was *way* more complicated than the flyer.

Suddenly there appeared bright blue lights around the opening of the bay. "The doors are fully open ... ready?"

"Maybe I shouldn't, sir, what if I mess up and crash?"

"You won't. I've been watching you ... you have the skills ... but if something scares you, just say 'your controls' and I'll take over. Remember, if I say 'my controls,' you let go of everything immediately!"

"Yes, sir." Karlson was terrified.

"Forward now ... slowly."

Karlson tipped the docking lever forward while watching the docking screen—ignoring the looming opening of the bay before them. Closer and closer they got. Karlson corrected the side distances, keeping the numbers around the screen equal. When the center number counted slowly down to zero, he put the drive lever to neutral. Then he took a deep breath ... so far, so good. He looked up. They were inside the hangar!

"Well done. Now push this button 'auto descend,' and the computer will turn us so that the shuttle faces outward and then it will lower us to the deck. We almost always use the 'computer-assist' for the final descent—to be sure that we don't land a bit crooked or too hard. Don't want to possibly damage anything!"

Karlson pushed the button; the craft turned 180 degrees and landed gently.

"Cut the artificial gravity ... cut the engine ... good. It was easy, right?" Palants grinned.

Karlson slumped down with relief. "I guess so, sir." Then he brightened, "Yes, sir, it was! Thank you for letting me learn!"

"Thank you, Junior Cadet, for being such a good student. Maybe when you're a bit older, we can train you to be a transport pilot ... that's where the real challenge is!" Then Sub-Commander Palants said wistfully, "I miss it. I hope the doctor will clear me for full duty when we get to our destination."

"Will your eye be OK?" Karlson dared to ask.

"The doctor says yes ... the patch comes off in a week or so ... I hope." He paused for a moment and then continued, "You know,

161

we all take life for granted ... even out here among the stars. We don't think that we could be wiped out of existence in a blink ... until we come face to face with it ... like I did. Now, I appreciate every moment, good and bad. I hope you understand what I'm saying ... value your life, and don't ever do anything unnecessarily risky, unless there is no other better choice."

"Yes, sir," Karlson promised.

Chapter 19

The Rear End

Karlson waited for Trace up on "F" deck, just outside the opening to the Dead Zone. They were going to compete with each other with their flips and somersaults. Trace had to do something before he could join him there, so Karlson put on a mag-belt and waited. He had been thinking about something from their lessons. The jets on the pressure suits used compressed gas to operate. As they expelled gas in airless, frictionless outer space, the action of the jet shooting out makes an equal and opposite reaction to the thing being pushed—the person in the suit. The gas shoots out, the person moves forward. If the reverse jets shoot out toward the front, the person in the suit slows, stops, and if the jet continues to release the compressed gas, the person in the suit moves backward.

He kept thinking about how the gas shoots out and the person moves. The Dead Zone did have air, but it was otherwise frictionless—nothing to slow you down. Expel gas ... propel forward. He wondered ....

It was time to try out his theory ... *before* Trace arrived. He flipped on the lights and entered the long cylindrical zero-gravity chamber. With a quick look to see if he were indeed alone in there, he let go of the hand-hold bar and floated, unmoving. He quickly pulled his pants down off his behind and let a big one! The sound thundered like a trumpet as it echoed down the chamber. To his surprise and immense satisfaction, he glided forward slightly! It worked!

* * *

At dinner, Sub-Commander Palants (no more eye-patch!) asked Karl if he would like Karlson to have another shuttle piloting lesson before the star-drive was engaged again. Karlson eagerly looked from Palants to his dad. Karl didn't even have to ask the boy; he knew that his son would be thrilled. So it was arranged.

*

Karlson met Sub-Commander Palants on the hangar deck, Bay 8. They entered the craft, and before the boy might ask, Palants pointed out their pressure suits hanging in the back. Karlson unsnapped two seat cushions from the jump seats and put them against the co-pilot seat backrest, and then he sat down. Palants grinned as he watched the boy.

"Don't worry, one day you'll grow enough to only need *one* cushion behind you," he teased.

"I hope so, sir."

"Do you remember how to call control?"

"Yes, sir, I think it is 'Hangar Control, Sub-Commander Pal ...'"

Palants interrupted him, "No, use *your* name."

"Oh," he was surprised. "Then it would be 'Hangar Control, Junior Cadet Karlson in Shuttle 8, requesting permission to disembark from Bay 8, for a duration of ...'" he looked at Palants.

"For less than an hour, like before. Ready?"

Karlson gulped his nervousness down, and tapped his microphone on. "Hangar Control, Junior Cadet Karlson in Shuttle 8 requesting permission to disembark from Bay 8, for a duration of less than an hour."

"Uh ... this is Hangar Control. Junior Cadet, are you alone?" the questioning voice replied over the radio.

"No, sir, Sub-Commander Palants is here and he is giving me a shuttle pilot lesson."

"In that case, Shuttle 8, permission granted."

Sub-commander Palants was chuckling the whole time. "My wife back home says I'm a tease, and my son agrees."

"You have a son?"

"Yes, and he is about your age. He is also a Junior Cadet at the Academy. Maybe when we get home, you'll meet him."

"Yes, sir, I would like that."

"Now, push this button here to start the airlock cycling process, but first tell control, 'Cycling.'"

Karlson tapped his microphone on and said "Cycling." Then he pushed the square button. The red lights flashed and the alarms sounded. Then the big hatch door behind them closed slowly to the deck. The air was pumped out, and the giant space doors opened before them.

"Now, tell me first what you need to do before you do it, and remember, if I say 'my control' you instantly lift up your hands and I will take over."

"Yes, sir, I remember ... first we turn on the artificial gravity."

"Good, do it."

"Then I use the docking controls to lift off?" he questioned.

"Yes, but this time the center number on the screen will start at zero and when it reaches ten, we will have cleared the bay."

So, Karlson moved the levers and their little craft rose and proceeded out of the hangar bay. He was careful to keep the numbers equal all around as they exited the starship. When the center number reached ten, he set the controls to neutral.

"Excellent. Now we switch to normal controls. Go forward to a distance of .001." Karlson moved the shuttle out to .001 on the readout, which was a good distance from the starship.

"Have you ever seen the back of the ship?" Palants asked.

"No, sir, just the front and the side."

"OK, let's go see the star-drive engines."

Karlson's eyes got big. "But sir, won't we get fried to a crisp if we go back there?" he asked anxiously.

Palants smiled, "If the star-drives were engaged, then yes, we would be fried to nothing but dust, maybe even less than that, but the star-drive is in neutral right now."

"I don't understand. Shouldn't it be 'on' since we are going somewhere?"

"No, what we do is power-drive until we reach a certain speed—about one light-year per day—then we put the star-drive to neutral, and sort of 'coast' along, until we need to slow down when we are nearing our destination. Then we turn the ship 180 degrees around and engage the star-drive engines again to slow us down.

"OK now, let's go. Gently turn and push your throttle just a bit, until we get behind the ship, then set the control to neutral."

Karlson did as directed, but still pondering his question, he asked "Why not just keep going faster and faster until the ship is half-way and then turn it around and use the star-drive to slow it?"

"That's a very good question, and there are some who would love to try it, but it's unsafe. You see, the sensors in the array can only see ahead but so far, and if we went faster than they can see, we would essentially be flying blind. We could crash into a planet or a star ... not good. One day, when the technology has been developed to see further ahead while at a greater speed, then we'll probably go faster."

"How fast can the starship go?"

"We honestly don't know. If you were in a car riding down the road on your planet, and if you lifted your foot off the power pedal, then the car would coast down slower and slower until it came to a stop, right?"

Karlson nodded.

"That's because the air in front of the car and the tires contacting the road give resistance—friction. Out here in space, there is no friction, so we would keep going and going. We power our ship with the star-drive until we reach a certain safe speed, then we put the drive at neutral, so we then coast along at that safe and constant speed. If we kept the star-drive engaged, we would go faster and faster and faster ... who knows how fast. Maybe some day we'll find out.

"OK, here we are at the back." Palants changed the subject. "Turn the shuttle so we are facing the rear of the ship."

Karlson did so, and there it was—the huge rear end of the ship! There were six massively huge circular star-drive engines arranged in a circle around the center hub. They were dark inside—thankfully! Outside of them, there was a ring of six smaller normal drive engines ports—also dark inside. Then outside of them was a ring of very large hangar space doors, marked C-1, C-2, and so on.

Karlson thought to himself: *So, this is the other end of the "hotdog bun," with the center hotdog hub, then the fat bun around it ... with the back of the bun having an inner ring of engines around the hotdog, then a second ring of engines, and then an outer ring of hangars around everything.*

"See C-1, C-2, and so on?" Palants pointed to the large hangar doors. "Those are the cargo bays. We don't use them unless we are loading cargo, and of course, when the star-drive is in neutral," Palants explained. Then he said mischievously, "Go ahead and cruise on over to the rear array—not too close, but closer than we are now."

Karlson inched the shuttle over so that the dome of the rear array was right in front of them. He thought to himself: *the back end of the hotdog!*

"Now wave!"

Karlson looked at Sub-Commander Palants like the man had lost his mind.

"Wave!" he said again, smiling as he waved to the array.

Feeling silly, Karlson also waved. Then all the lights on the end of the huge ship came on and then blinked on and off. "They're waving back!" Palants laughed.

"They are!" Karlson said excitedly as they both waved even harder.

Then the radio came on, "We see you, Shuttle 8, so we won't turn on the engines at this time ..."

Karlson could hear laughter in the background. Then Palants tapped on his microphone, "Thank you, Control, we very much appreciate that."

* * *

The day was July 15, Karlson's chosen birthday. His dad wished him a happy 12th, and asked if he would like the cooks to make him a birthday cake. Karlson said no, emphatically. He didn't want anyone else to know it was his birthday, especially Trace. He had heard that sometimes people would spank you the number of years of your birthday, and add one smack on for good luck, or something like that. He didn't want to give Trace even the *idea* of spanking him, not because he thought his friend would actually hurt him, but because it would be humiliating. Birthday parties were always a good idea, but this spanking thing—not so much. So, Karlson's 12th birthday was a non-event, which was just fine with him.

The *Seeker* turned 180 degrees around, and the great star-drive engines were engaged. They needed to slow down as they approached the area of the strange power surge that was the reason for this new voyage. Long range sensors picked up their destination—it was a planet.

Chapter 20

R. I. P.

It was quiet in the control room. Mapping was probably the most boring job on the ship, especially during 3rd shift when most everyone was asleep. The Airman's job was to watch the viewscreens of the video feeds from the drones as they made their mapping passes over the planet surface. He was the only person there except for one other officer way over at the other end of the large control room complex.

The planet was nothing but a big cold airless rock. He was so bored that he had brought along a hand-held video game ... and he was winning. He glanced up at the six viewscreens as something flashed by. He quickly put down the game, and reversed the view feed. Rectangles! Millions of rectangles! He tasked a seventh special drone to go to the place of rectangles for a low altitude view. He couldn't believe what he was seeing! He quickly put the game in his pocket. If he had missed this while playing a stupid game while on duty, jeopardizing his career ... he couldn't even dare think of the consequences! He mentally scolded himself and vowed to never ever be derelict in his work again.

He called the other officer over to show him the pictures, then *he* woke the Captain. It was amazing. Close-up views showed thousands of rows of rectangles ... and within each rectangle, there was a body.

*

Everyone on the ship was excited over this extraordinarily rare find. Another planet with definite signs of intelligent life! Low passes with the drone cameras gave very close-up and detailed pictures of the bodies lying within their rectangles. They seemed to be dead—at least they didn't move any as the drones hovered above them. The High Commander must have been in a very good mood as he allowed Junior Cadet Karlson to accompany the first explorer group going to the surface of the mysterious planet.

Commander Karl, Karlson, and eight other people were going, including some lady scientists. The rock-like planet was virtually airless, so there would obviously be no air pressure, therefore the team wore pressure suits.

The group assembled at hangar Bay 12. When everyone had arrived, they entered the transport ship, but it was nothing like the transports that Karlson had ridden on before! It was totally stripped down. Gone were the neat rows of plush seats and carpet; instead there were metal seat slots lined up along the sides, and a bright metal deck. The scientific instruments they would be using were stowed down the center of the ship, tied securely to the deck. There wasn't even a wall between them and the transport pilots that sat high up at the front of the craft.

Knowing his son had questions, Karl explained that this was a special transport, used for missions to new planets, where unknown and unseen dangers might exist—like pathogens such as microbes, bacteria, viruses—or anything alien. After their exploration, the transport and the team's pressure suits would have to be decontaminated before the hangar doors of Bay 12, the de-con area, would open to the rest of the ship. Every precaution must be taken to *not* possibly bring back anything that could contaminate the ship and the people in it.

After everyone was seated into their oversized slots (that allowed for the cumbersome pressure suits), the transport hatch door was sealed, the hangar door closed, the air was pumped out, and then the doors to space opened. The transport gently lifted off and exited the starship. There was a viewscreen at the front of the "passenger" section, so everyone had a great view of the strange dead planet as they approached it. In just 10 minutes, the pilots set the big transport gently on the planet surface, within easy walking distance to the first row of bodies.

"Helmets on!" came the voice of the team leader, senior science officer Commander Stock. At all "green lights," the cabin was depressurized and the hatch door opened onto a new world.

The gravity on this planet was a little less than what the crew considered "normal," so it was easier to walk even with the heavy packs on their pressure suit backs. There was little light, like at dusk, because this planet was so far from its sun. They cautiously walked across the firm black ground toward the first rectangle. As they approached, it became evident that the rectangles were huge! They lined up next to the first one and stood in awe. The body inside was every bit of 20 feet tall!

"With your permission, Commander Stock," Karl's voice said over the helmet radios, "I would like the Junior Cadet to describe what he sees and what he can discern from his observations."

"Very well, Commander," Stock's voice answered, then said to the boy. "Well, Junior Cadet, what do you see? And what are your preliminary conclusions based on your observations?"

Karlson suspected, since his lessons included "Analytical Thought," that his father would probably ask him to describe what he saw in order to hone his observation skills, so he was somewhat prepared. He just wasn't prepared to do it now in front of all the scientists! He stood at the end of the rectangle (that came up to his chest) and looked at the strange creature within. But instead of 'Wow! What a monster!' he started his description with a deep breath and the facts. "Sir, I see an alien being—not human—possibly 20 feet tall, lying in what appears to be an open casket, because the being seems to be dead."

"Continue," senior science officer Commander Stock said.

"The being appears to be somewhat ... insect looking, but with two feet and two arms, and one head. The feet are covered with some kind of boots—black, and the legs are covered with a skirt going down to the boots. The skirt, or robe, is also black but with alternating gold and silver bands on it, going in a diagonal pattern."

The others backed away some to let him pass as he walked along the long side of the casket toward the head. "The upper body is covered with a heavier material ... like light armor, maybe. It is a blue color with gold flecks ... somewhat ornamental looking. The hands have claws—maybe four claws on each hand—and they are crossed across the chest, and holding the hilt of the biggest sword I've ever seen! It must be 8 or 10 feet long!" He paused, admiring the sword, and then continued, "The head is the most unusual. It looks like an insect face. It is pale gray, and appears to have two big eyes, closed with eyelids, and slits for a nose. It must have a mouth, but I can't see it very well. The head has a metal looking helmet on it, and I don't see any hair. There seems to be thousands, maybe millions, of these beings all lined up in neat rows, like we saw from the ship." He turned toward Commander Stock, "Sir, I think this place is a cemetery."

"Why do you say that?"

"Because sir, they are all laid out in their nice clothes, I guess, and in rows. And they are *dead*, sir."

"What makes you think they are dead? Might this species sometimes go dormant, as in hibernation, to revive later?"

Karlson hadn't thought of that as he peered closely at the alien face ... half expecting the big bug eyes to suddenly open. On movies the monsters do that; they appear to be dead, and then they pop up and get you!

"No, sir, I think the facts indicate that they are dead. There is no air here, so they couldn't breathe, and they appear to have nose slits so they probably *do* need to breathe. Even hibernating animals breathe. Also, sir, because there is no atmosphere here, decomposition would be greatly slowed, therefore preserving the bodies for their fellow beings to visit, if they do that—which I suspect they might because of the way the bodies are displayed."

"Excellent preliminary analysis, Junior Cadet! Very well done. But I have some additional questions for you. How do you know these are intelligent beings? Perhaps these bodies are *pets* of a superior race, and this is a pet cemetery?"

Stunned at the question, Karlson thought a moment before answering. "No, sir, we can't know for sure, but that isn't likely because pets—as we know them—do not carry weapons aside from the ones that they are born with. And if these beings are not pets, they must be intelligent because they are here, on this planet ... and we have mapped the planet, and there is nothing else here, so they had to get here by space travel unless they live *inside* the planet and come out here to leave their dead."

"Good, but we have analyzed the planet and it's solid. So, if these are not pets, and are indeed intelligent beings, are they more likely peaceful or warlike?"

Karlson looked at the big sword closely. "I think, sir, that they are more likely to be warlike, because the sword blade appears very sharp, and their clothing appears military-ish. If the sword were dull, I would think it might be more ceremonial, instead of useful. And they have it in their coffins with them, which indicates military honors."

"I concur completely," Commander Stock agreed. "They might very well be technologically advanced—more advanced than we are—because they most likely left the powerful energy pulse that brought us here to investigate. And if they are indeed more advanced, and warlike instead of peaceful, then I hope we don't run into them in the future ... even though it would be a great scientific experience."

Karlson stood aside while the scientists and crew took pictures and measurements of the giant creature. They set up a portable x-ray machine to examine the body's internal organs. They took small samples of the clothing, but otherwise did not disturb the giant in its coffin. Several scientists walked down the long row of bodies, looking for some differences in appearance or dress, but they all seemed the same. When they were done with their scientific tests and readings, they boarded the transport, took off, but landed again at a spot far away from the first body.

The bodies at the new spot appeared to be "dryer," or less fresh, than the first one. The body they had first examined was most likely recently deceased, whereas the others had been there a great deal longer. It confirmed the hypothesis that this planet was indeed, a cemetery.

One of the scientists said as they were leaving, "R. I. P."

Karlson asked, "Sir, what does 'R. I. P.' mean?"

"It means 'Rest In Peace.' You say that to dead people."

"Oh," Karlson said. "They look like they are."

*

When the team arrived back at the starship, they had to go through decontamination. All the people went into a special chamber, put their helmet sun visors down, spread their arms out and turned slowly while the de-con "lights" shown on every part of their pressure suits. While they were being "sterilized," the special transport was decontaminated as well, inside and out, plus the hangar bay itself. Safety is everything.

*

Everyone was talking about the amazing find on the rock planet. Soon the beings were nicknamed Bug-men. It wasn't very flattering, but it fit.

Chapter 21

Ocean World

There were four planets in the solar system. The farthest one from that sun was the Bug-men cemetery, and the second was another lifeless rock. As always, it was mapped, and then the starship continued to the third planet. As they approached, this planet seemed different; it appeared to be all ocean! Not a speck of land anywhere! It was quite lovely, like a great blue jewel hanging in space. Preliminary readings were taken, and it appeared that the planet had a breathable atmosphere, a normal gravity, and a barely slightly above normal air pressure. After mapping (which showed the land *under* the ocean), the stripped down transport traveled to the planet. Since it couldn't land, it hovered above the surface of the water as the scientists took more precise readings and samples of the water.

Karlson, after his usual lessons with Trace, hung around the laboratories where the testing of the atmosphere and water samples were being conducted. One of the scientists, who had been on the mission to the Bug-men cemetery, saw him and invited him in. She and the other scientists explained their testing procedures, and Karlson paid rapt attention. Senior science officer Commander Stock was impressed with the boy's interest.

Results of the tests confirmed that the planet was safe (as far as they could tell) to go back to without wearing protective gear. So, a shuttle was specially prepared so it could land on the water surface. Karlson went to the hangar bay where the shuttle was being fitted with pontoons. He had never seen pontoons before. They were big, fat, long balloon like things that were attached to the shuttle's struts, so that it would float on the water. In fact, the pontoons made the shuttle so fat at the bottom, it had to be first moved from its normal hangar bay to a larger bay because it would have been too wide to make it through the space doors!

Commander Karl was to be team leader on this mission, so he obtained the High Commander's permission for Karlson to come along. Everyone dressed in their "warm weather" uniforms, since the temperatures at their destination near the equator would be like a summer day.

*

The shuttle pilot flew over the surface of the water, and finding it relatively calm, he carefully landed. The pontoons made the landing "odd," as the shuttle moved gently up and down with the movement of the water below.

The scientists opened the large hatch door from which they would collect more water samples and drop cameras into the ocean. The weather was so warm that they also opened the smaller hatch door on the other side of the shuttle. Karlson asked if he could sit at the smaller hatch where he could still watch the scientists on the inside, but also look out over the ocean—this way he would be out of the way. Karl gave permission, as long as the boy wore a safety harness. As his dad fitted the contraption of straps over the boy's body, through the open hatch Karlson could see the blue ocean that was without end.

Karlson held onto the hand rail as he sat down on the deck at the edge of the hatch door. He was about to snap his harness tether hook over the anchor bracket at his side, when a sudden wave raised one end of the shuttle. Everyone was caught off guard and toppled over ... everyone but him—he flipped right out of the hatch and bounced off the pontoon!

Karlson was surprised to suddenly find himself under water! He was a bit stunned from the bounce, but otherwise unhurt. He reached up for the water surface but instead found only the cold rubber of a pontoon. Panic! He had to breathe! He clawed at the never ending clammy rubber. Need air! Need air! Finally he cleared the barrier and his head popped through to the surface. Air! He took a giant deep breath and then sputtered and spit while treading the cool water to stay afloat. He twisted around to see where he was.

"Karlson!" his father yelled. "Karlson!"

Karl leapt from the hatch onto the pontoon and collapsed onto his stomach. "Karlson, where are you!" He looked and saw nothing. His fear grew. "Karlson!" He was just about to enter the water when he heard a sound.

"I'm OK, Dad," a small voice came from the water.

"Where are you!" Karl frantically searched again over the edge of the pontoon. "I can't see you!"

"I'm under the shuttle!" the boy called back.

Karl spun around and peered through the space between the shuttle struts and the pontoon. "I see you! Son, can you swim to the front of the shuttle? I can lift you up there—at the end of the pontoon."

"OK!" Karlson answered, and started to swim.

Karl half crawled and half slithered across the wet bouncy pontoon surface until he reached the front end.

Then the boy's voice nervously called from the shadowy underside of the shuttle. "D-Dad! There's ... there's something down here!"

Karl had lifted his son out of the water. After assuring everyone that he was OK, Karlson climbed back into the shuttle. He was dripping wet from head to toe, but the air was so warm that he dried quickly.

"You said something was down there; what did you mean?"

"What did you see?"

"Did you hit your head?"

Karlson was peppered with questions.

"I didn't hit my head. I saw a thing ... a creature. I just saw it for an instant before it went back down under the water. It was actually ... kind of cute."

"What did it look like?"

Karlson took a deep breath, "It had a round head with big blue eyes; that's all I saw."

"What color was it?"

"Can you draw it?"

The questions flew at him.

Then a scientist said barely over a whisper, "Ladies and gentlemen, look over here ...."

Just a few feet beyond the pontoon were three little heads bobbing up and down with the small waves of the water. They were green with two big blue eyes ... that blinked sideways! They had little heart shaped mouths, but no nose. As they bobbed a bit closer, the scientists could see that they had gills, like a fish, opening and closing on the sides of their necks as the water lapped over them. They were so cute!

Then they were gone. The scientists scrambled to review the video footage from the cameras that were in the water. The video showed little bodies with two arms that had hands, but the rest of their bodies were like fish. Mermaids! The whole creature appeared to be around two feet tall ... or long.

Everyone was astounded. The rest of the afternoon proved to be uneventful as the little water creatures did not reappear. The cameras were pulled up and then attached to large floatation devices, so they could be left hanging in the water after the shuttle left, to send back continuous video.

The rotation of the ocean planet was faster than normal, so night approached sooner than usual. The hatches were secured and the shuttle left the planet. All evening and through the night, video from the underwater cameras was shown throughout the ship's viewscreens. It proved to be quite a show, as the little creatures came back and swam around them, touching them. Even though they couldn't possibly know what the cameras were for, one creature held onto one of them and seemed to make faces at it! It was truly amazing.

*

The next day, the shuttle returned to the water surface where the cameras were floating. Karlson had successfully asked to go along, after promising to attach his harness to the bracket *before* he sat down in the opening. They waited and waited, but the little creatures were nowhere—either above or below the water surface.

About an hour had passed and Karlson sat with his eyes half closed, daydreaming in the warm sunshine as he sat with one leg inside and the other leg dangling over the side of the shuttle hatch opening. He heard a little splash. There they were! Three little heads! Trying not to make any sudden moves, he whispered, "They're back!"

The rest of the shuttle crew silently moved over and stood behind him, watching the little water beings. Then, to the amazement of everyone, one little creature swam over to the pontoon, reached up, and quickly put a brightly colored shell on it. Then it swam backward, watching. The second creature did the same! Then the third one swam over, but because it was a bit smaller than the others, when it tried to place its shell, it slid off. The little creature quickly disappeared under the water and then reappeared with the shell. It seemed to go under again, but then jumped up out of the water and successfully placed its shell next to the other two. Then it swam backward to join the others. There they stayed, watching the shuttle with their sideways blinking, big blue eyes.

One of the scientists hung out over the pontoon and with protective gloves, collected the shells. One was a bright blue, one was red, and one was yellow. As they marveled excitedly over the shells, Karlson studied the little creatures. They seemed to be waiting, with their big eyes blinking more rapidly ... almost expectantly. Remembering his time living on the streets, he blurted out, "I think the water babies want to trade!"

"Water babies! So, you have given them a name," one person said.

"You think they want to trade? Why?" Karl asked

"Because that's how *we* did it. We put out something where we knew another gang was, and we waited to see if they were interested. Then we would talk and trade."

The team looked at the waiting water babies.

"And," Karlson continued, "because we have taken their trade shells, they are expecting three things in return!"

Not really thinking it through, the crew began hunting for things to give. One lady scientist had a small plastic-edged unbreakable mirror that she had in her pocket. Another person found a plastic brush with stiff bristles. They needed one more thing. Karlson held up a strap with two snap rings, one on each end. Everyone agreed that these things were good, so before anyone could stop him, Karlson slipped out of the hatch and down onto the pontoon (he had his harness on). He turned to gather the three trade items and then carefully walked across the bouncy pontoon as far as the harness would allow, and sat down. He put the items in a row in front of him, and waited. While he waited, he demonstrated how the items worked. He hooked the strap to itself and then unhooked it, stretching it out. He pretended to scrub the pontoon with the brush. He looked into the mirror, plus he held it outward to them.

With their big blue eyes sideways blinking wildly, the water babies cautiously approached him. He sat as still as he could, as they swam nearer and nearer. He could see them plainly; they were so close. They had a little ridge across the top of their heads that ran down their backs. Their green skin looked smooth, not scaly. He could barely hear it, but they seemed to make little chirping noises. Their bright blue eyes watched him as one by one, they snatched an item off the pontoon.

Trade accepted.

They swam several yards away from the shuttle to examine their prizes. The mirror seemed to make the biggest impression, as they passed the items between themselves. It seemed that it was decided who got what, and the smallest got the strap. The water baby played with it, but seemed frustrated, so it swam back to Karlson—holding out the strap. It touched one end of the snap ring to the other, but they did not hook. It blinked at Karlson and held the strap up to him. The harness kept Karlson from reaching the strap, so he quickly unhooked the tether from it. He reached out and took the strap from the brave little water baby. He leaned over and showed the water baby how to put his thumb on the side of the ring, pushing the latch open, and then put the two ends together. He then did the same, showing how to unhook them. The water baby watched, fascinated. Karlson then held it out to the little creature, who took it and opened the ring easily, hooked them together, then unhooked them. It looked up at

Karlson and their eyes met. They each held their gaze with the other—it was as if the little creature was thanking him. Then it disappeared beneath the water. The other two were gone as well.

Karlson re-hooked the tether to the harness before his watching dad would notice, he hoped. He waited, but the little water babies did not return.

*

Since they couldn't stay forever at the ocean world, it was decided to place more floating cameras in various positions across the planet, and set up a signal booster in space to re-broadcast (to headquarters) any images that the cameras picked up. Their last stop was back at the place where they had made the trade. The shuttle landed on the gentle waves, and Karlson took his usual position sitting at the edge of the hatch door with his legs hanging over the side. It only took a few minutes before the three cute little heads appeared. As they swam toward the shuttle, it appeared that they had more shells to trade. Suddenly, two more heads broke the surface of the water behind them. These were *not* water babies! The two were obviously of the same species as the little ones, but they seemed every bit as big as the Star People!

Everyone in the shuttle watched in hushed silence as the two quietly approached the water babies from behind. Karlson pulled his legs slowly inside the shuttle. He feared for the little water babies! Suddenly the two large beings attacked the babies! Unthinking, Karlson jumped up. "What do we do!"

"Wait!" exclaimed one of the lady scientists. "Look!"

The two big water creatures had hold of the three little ones, but the little ones were not struggling. The eyes of the large creatures were sideways blinking furiously, and the chirping noises they made were loud enough for the anxious crew to hear plainly. Then one of the large creatures turned to swim off along with the water babies, but the smallest baby did not follow. The same large creature turned and grabbed the hand of the remaining baby and then the four of them disappeared beneath the waves. The other large creature stared at the crew in the shuttle; its eyes now seldom blinking. It slowly swam a bit closer. Then it held up what appeared to be a spear! It glared at the crew, then suddenly turned and disappeared into the deep.

The lady scientist started laughing! Everyone turned to her. "Don't you see?" she laughed. "Those two were the *parents*! They were angry because their children were *talking to strangers*!"

*

That evening on the ship, the videos taken by the shuttle crew were shown on the viewscreens. Everyone loved the cute little water babies. When the scene where Karlson unhooked his tether flashed by, Karl leaned over to his son and said, "I saw that."

Karlson grimaced and then grinned awkwardly and said, "I hoped you wouldn't notice."

Karl sighed, "Well, I did … but I get it. You needed to get closer to the little ones. I guess I can't keep you totally safe every minute of every day. Little boys grow up to be men, and you are well on your way."

The video changed to the last encounter with the mermaid people. As the crew watched the adults scold the children, everyone chuckled. The expression of "the more things change, the more they stay the same" was so true. They were on another planet, and here the parents told their children to beware of strangers just the same as human parents do!

Chapter 22

Space Travel Can Be Boring

The time it took to travel between stars and between planets in a star's solar system could be boring, and often was. Trace made a real effort to keep Karlson's lessons as interesting as he could, but there was only so much he could do. He often added jokes or riddles.

His latest: "Why did the starship cross the galaxy?"

Karlson answered, "To seek out and explore ...."

"No! To get to the other side!" Trace laughed hysterically.

Karlson just rolled his eyes and then frowned, "That's just stupid, and anyway, isn't it supposed to be 'why did the *chicken* cross the *road*?'"

"Yeah, but that's the old way, this is the new way!" Trace said, still grinning.

"Either way, it's still just plain dumb."

"Yeah, it's dumb, but the look on your face—it was worth it!"

Occasionally Karlson felt like he was older than Trace.

*

Sometimes Karlson and Trace would go to the gym. Sometimes they would go to the laser pistol range. Sometimes they would goof off in the Dead Zone. In spite of the occasional dumb riddles, Trace was a good guy, and Karlson liked him a lot.

And then sometimes, Sub-Commander Palants took Karlson out for additional piloting lessons in the shuttle. The boy was a "natural," showing excellence in the skills needed for a good pilot. He let Karlson sit in the pilot seat while he, in the co-pilot seat, pretended to take a nap.

There was one more planet in the Bug-men and Ocean World solar system. It was the one closest to the solar system's star. It was a small, lifeless rock world. While it was being mapped, Palants obtained permission from the Captain and the High Commander to give Karlson his only remaining lesson in the shuttle: how to land on a non-ship surface—like a planet.

Karlson was a little bit nervous as they approached the barren landscape of the rock-like planet. Because there was no atmosphere to cause friction, the readout on the hull temperature remained low ... until they flew out of the shadow of the planet and into the bright sunlight. Palants was in the pilot seat as he explained new things.

"Because we are so close to the sun, the temperature on the hull will rise very quickly, and can be very dangerous. See? Check the hull temp display. See how fast it is rising? Now, let's go back into the shadow of the planet. Now, see how the temp is reducing? This little shuttle can take a lot, but we don't want to push it, so we'll stay on the cold side, which, in case you are wondering, is *very* cold, even this close to the sun!"

Karlson nodded in agreement. He remembered his lessons.

"I have a riddle for you!" Palants grinned.

Oh, no, not you too! Trace is bad enough! Karlson thought, but he said politely, "Sir?"

"OK, what is the temperature of outer space?" he asked teasingly.

"That's easy sir. It is really hot, like millions of degrees, or really cold, like near absolute zero where nothing moves, not even molecules or atoms ... or somewhere in-between." Karlson answered confidently.

"Wrong!" Palants laughed. "Outer space has *no* temperature at all! Because outer space is *nothing* at all! It's what is *in* outer space that has a temperature. If something is close to a sun (a heat source), it can be millions of degrees hot, and if something is far, far away from a sun or in a shadow, it can be extremely cold, like you said. You know, cold is nothing more than the absence of heat on something, but it has to be on *something*." Palants chuckled, "It's a trick question."

"Yes, sir, I get it, and it *is* a trick question!" Karlson smiled. He would try to trick Trace with that one.

"Now, let's land. In an atmosphere, we would monitor the hull temperature as we descend, because our speed through it would cause friction and the temperature would rise. The atmosphere can also cause us to be knocked around with air turbulence, but that is not an issue today—because there's no air. We are going to land without computer-assist. So, see the readout on the altimeter? That's how far off the ground we are. Right now it reads in whole numbers, but when we get really close, it will read distance with a whole number and a one place decimal. See? It reads 20, so we are about 20 feet off the ground. Watch while we go down."

Karlson watched the altimeter. As their small craft descended, the numbers counted down. When the readout reached 10, the numbers went to 9.9, 9.8, and so on.

"Here is something nice," Palants said as he flipped a switch next to the altimeter. Suddenly a synthetic voice spoke out loud the numbers of the altimeter! "This is really helpful when we're landing on a less than flat surface, where we have to carefully watch the ground as we approach."

When the shuttle was less than one foot off the ground and descending even slower, the synthetic voice readout said ".9" and so on until it said "contact," as they felt the strut rails gently touch the surface of the rocky planet.

"See?" Palants asked. "Normally we don't land *quite* that slowly until we get to the last couple of feet. I just wanted you to get the feel of it. So, let's go up again and *you* land this time!"

They lifted off and traveled a bit to another location. Karlson took the controls, leaving the audible countdown on. He landed perfectly. Then Palants said, "Let's go up again, and you land again, but this time, with your eyes closed."

Karlson was stunned. "Sir, with my eyes *closed*?"

"Yes, to give you the experience of landing by instruments only, like if it were at night and your landing lights were malfunctioning. See this topography screen? It shows the land below, whether it is flat or bumpy. You always want to choose the flattest area, obviously. Now, without looking out the viewport, use the topography screen to pick your landing area."

Karlson, nervous with this new procedure, watched the screen until the area below showed a flat surface. "Here, sir."

"Good, now close your eyes and start your descent. Don't worry, I'll take over if necessary," Palants said with confidence.

Karlson closed his eyes and started the descent, listening to the synthetic voice call out the distance to the surface. Down they went.

"You're doing great," Palants reassured him.

".8, .5, .2," the machine voice called out. Karlson was landing the craft extremely slowly, and then he felt the skids touch the surface just as the voice said, "Contact."

"Whew!" Karlson breathed with relief.

"You did just fine. See, it wasn't that scary, was it?"

"I guess not, sir, but let's *not* do it again."

Palants just chuckled.

*

Even the Captain must have been getting bored, because he announced a contest—a contest for best shot on the laser range. The prize was three days of no duty, which was actually pretty funny, because everyone didn't have enough to do already— that's why the boredom! Regardless, everybody entering the contest wanted to win. Trace and Karlson spent extra time at the range, as did almost everyone else. Trace even spent time there when Karlson *wasn't* with him.

Trace had an idea ... "Hey kid, why don't we put on a little show? You know, with our jumps and rolls while we shoot!"

He had Karlson's attention. "Do you think the Captain would want us to? Or would we just look silly?"

"I don't think we would look silly at all. In most dangerous situations, we would most likely be on the move, not always standing still like most people do at the range. I'll ask the Captain."

*

As it turned out, the Captain *loved* the idea! He said it showed creativity, and he liked that in the crew. So, Karlson and Trace practiced a routine. Sometimes they got up early and sometimes they practiced late ... just so no one else would know what they were up to, except for Karl ... Karlson did not keep secrets from his dad.

*

The day arrived for the contest. Everyone in the crew was excited—it didn't take much when you are bored to death. A camera was set up to broadcast the trials throughout the ship. First, each person who wanted to participate shot ten times at a target. Anyone who did not hit the target within the center ring was disqualified. Then the second trial used a smaller target, and then those who did not hit the center ring were disqualified. The third trial eliminated all but ten people. Both Trace and Karlson were still in the competition, as was Karl and seven others.

The Captain, High Commander, and the Pistol Range Master were the final judges. Nearly everyone was watching the final competition on the viewscreens throughout the ship, except for those few on critical duty. The Pistol Range Master stood up in front of the group assembled in the pistol range (and the cameras) and said, "We have a special treat for you this afternoon, before we have the final competition. It's a demonstration of combat moves under fire, presented to us by our two youngest officers onboard, Junior Airman Trace and Junior Cadet Karlson. Let's give them a hand!" And then he started clapping. Everyone else also started clapping as Trace and Karlson walked to the front.

"Yeah!" they called out. "Give us a good show!" Everyone was in a great mood.

"Ready?" Trace glanced at Karlson.

"Ready!" Karlson answered with more confidence than he really felt.

Their music started. (They chose to have music in order to better time their movements.) Trace dropped to one knee and Karlson jumped behind him and with both hands on the pistol, he took aim over Trace's shoulder. They both fired together at a hideous monster face that popped up. (Karlson had drawn them!) Zap zap! It was a pretty big target so they both easily nailed it. Then Trace dropped to the deck and rolled over while Karlson went to one knee. In unison, they both shot at another hideous monster face that popped up. Zap zap! Got it! Then Karlson dropped to the deck and together they both rolled twice and took aim from the deck at another ugly thing that popped up. Bingo!

Trace jumped up and hopped over Karlson as he rolled over twice. Then they both again shot in unison. Dead monster! Karlson rolled twice back again as Trace jumped over him again. Fire! Got it! Then Trace hopped over top of Karlson (who was still on the deck), with one foot on one side and his other foot on the other side of the boy. Together they fired. Direct hits!

Then Trace put his pistol in the holster on his belt, reached down, grabbed Karlson's wrists and quickly pulled him up from the deck into a standing position in front of himself. Trace reached for and drew the pistols (he had two!) from the holsters on his belt, and together they fired at a new target that had just popped up. It was a big circle with a curved line at the bottom. Zap zap zap! Two side-by-side marks on top made by Trace and one mark in the middle made by Karlson. They had made a smiley face!

They both were a little out of breath as they turned to their audience. Everyone was clapping and hollering! "Yeah!" "That was great!" "Whooop, whooop!" "Alright!"

Karlson and Trace both grinned as they ridiculously bowed hugely and flamboyantly to the cheers.

*

The final competition began. Each person had three shots. Both Karl and Karlson did well, but Trace and one other person made it to the final two contestants. As they waited for the special target to be set up, Trace looked at his competitor. "Do you work in the galley?" he asked the slightly overweight man standing next to him.

"Yes, I'm the guy who makes the biscuits and gravy that you always get two helpings of," he smiled.

"I thought so," Trace smiled back. "That is the best tasting stuff I have ever had!"

"You can thank my great-grandmother; it was her recipe."

"Well, my thanks to her," Trace laughed. "I ought to *let* you win because of great-granny's talent."

"No thanks, buddy, do your best!"

Then the Range Master said, "Ready? Junior Airman Trace, you go first."

Trace took careful aim, and fired three shots. They were all within the small circle on the target.

The cook grimaced. "That's awesome. This is going to be tough."

"Do your best, man. It's only a game."

The cook took his aim and fired. Two of the shots were nearly dead center, but the third shot was barely outside the circle.

The Range Master took down the targets and gave them to the other judges. After only a few moments of discussion, the Captain stood up and said, "Excellent shooting from all the semi-finalists and especially to you both, our two finalists. It was a tough call, but the judges here are in agreement. Junior Airman Trace, you are the winner!"

Everyone slapped Trace on the back and shook his hand. They congratulated the cook as well. Trace went to him and offered his hand, "Great job. How did you get so good?"

"Lived on a farm when I was a kid," the cook explained. "We shot cans off a fence rail ... then we went to the kitchen to stuff ourselves with great-grandma's gravy biscuits!"

Chapter 23

Beautiful World

The *Seeker* was on its way to another star. Using the star-drive, it still took three months to reach it. The new solar system had six planets. The first was a barren rock with an atmosphere, but it was un-breathable. The ship stayed a week to take samples and map it, then traveled to the next planet. From a distance, it didn't look any more interesting than the first—and it wasn't. Then the ship left to map the third planet, which *did* look promising, and the closer they got, the more excited the scientists and crew became. As always, when encountering a new planet, the most interesting images were broadcast throughout the ship's viewscreens. In the past, most images were somewhat boring, but this time, everyone (not on duty) was fascinated by them. The planet was beautiful. The oceans were a greenish-blue ... a soft aqua color. Of the two landmasses, one was mostly green and the other was green and white. Upon closer examination, the white places were actually cities. Another world of intelligent beings! Everyone was beside themselves with amazement and anticipation.

*

The ship dropped into a low orbit and, using the highest settings, the cameras revealed a wonderful world. The vegetation in the fields and forests was a bright vibrant green, and the cities were gleaming pure white. The mapping drones were sent out. Close-up views showed tall spires on the buildings—some seemingly solid and some of delicate filigree—and all with tips of gold. Mapping took longer than usual, as the drones were tasked to do more intricate closer examinations. Throughout that time something strange was noticed ... there was no evidence of anything moving on the planet's surface—no land vehicles, no ships, no aircraft. At night, there were no lights in any city ... and there were thousands of cities. The stunningly beautiful world seemed deserted.

After the usual tests were finished, it appeared that the air was breathable, air pressure was normal, and the surface temperatures were comfortable (like an early fall day). Gravity was slightly less than normal, and no unusual pathogens were evidenced. Because the boy had shown such interest in the scientific routine testing before, senior science officer Commander Stock obtained permission from the High Commander and Karl for Karlson to join them.

*

As per protocol, until further and more exacting pathogen tests were made of the soil and surface atmosphere, safety required protective gear. So, the first visit to the planet surface involved the stripped-down transport and crew in protective suits—but this time in air-suits. These suits were different from pressure suits. They were much lighter and the gloves were not so clumsy. They still had helmets and back packs, but these back packs were for *positive* air flow (air produced in the suit, and constantly expelled *out* of the suit, therefore never letting any air from the alien environment *into* the suit).

The team stripped down to their underwear and put on the air-suits. Karl had ordered several of these at the same time he had ordered the boy's pressure suits, so Karlson fit into his perfectly. His air tank pack was attached, but being full size, it was a bit heavy for a boy.

Everyone walked to hangar Bay 12 and entered the stripped-down transport and sat in the cold metal slot seats. Sub-Commander Palants was already onboard in the pilot seat, and waved to Karlson as he entered the craft.

They waited patiently while the ship was sealed and the airlock cycled, then they were on their way! Sub-Commander Palants landed the transport in a green grassy field just outside one of the largest cities. Everyone exited the craft except for the pilots. Each person was laden with heavy testing equipment, except for Karlson—his air tank was heavy enough.

Karlson looked toward the city. The beautiful white spires towered majestically into the sky, and the sunlight sparkled off their golden tips. The wide entrance to the city was framed with a huge arch of white stone, and edged with intricately carved white filigree. The city looked like it could be home to winged fairies and elves—almost magical!

Karlson wanted to go explore, but since the scientists were the ones who had invited him on this first landing on the new planet, he visited each one as they performed their tests. As he watched, they seemed very pleased at their readings. This first visit on the planet surface was short, only about 2 hours. All the samples were stowed properly, and the small team re-entered the transport and returned to the starship. Their preliminary test results seemed to confirm that the new world would be safe to explore without protective suits, but they wouldn't have final results until the next morning.

Back at the ship, when they exited the transport they had to go through decontamination, just as before. Karlson was excited about possibly going with the next team—the exploring team that would go *into* the magical city. At dinner, he told his dad all about what he had seen, and asked to go again. Karl said that he would not be able to go with the first exploration team into the city, but if all went well, he could go in the second ... because Karl would be team leader on that one.

*

The results came back "positive" for safety, and the first exploration team went to the planet surface. It was a large team of about 40 people. Karlson was glued to the viewscreen as they sent back video of what they were finding. The city seemed to have a low decorative wall around its entirety, but a wall that would not keep anything out, or in ... it was just pretty with lattice and filigree.

The city was quite large, over twenty miles in approximate diameter. There were many parks with nice white walkways, benches, and gazebos—large and small. Vegetation in the main part of the city was mostly confined within the parks and in numerous large containers set among the buildings and lining the streets. Smaller buildings, perhaps homes, had areas of land in back of them, like back yards, and some had small front yards. Everything was clean and white, like the entire city had just been scrubbed. It looked almost brand new ... everything but the vegetation—most of it was unkempt and overgrown with weeds. The city was still beautiful, but at times past with green grass, flowers, and blooming trees, it must have been absolutely stunning.

Along the streets were parked white and gold land vehicles. They were sleek in design with large passenger areas inside. The building doors were about 15 feet high. Some buildings seemed to be for social events or governmental use, others were shops. Off the main streets were many side streets and off them were homes. Inside the homes were furniture and beds ... seemingly for a race of people who stood around 10 feet tall. Then there were the photos ... of families. The people were quite humanoid, but tall and thin. They had golden colored skin and smooth limbs, with hands of 6 long delicate fingers each. Their faces were elegant, with beautiful almond shaped eyes, slender noses, and delicate smiling lips. Their hair was pure white, and like the beautiful cities they had built, they too were strangely beautiful.

But, where were these people? It appeared that they had just gotten up and vanished. Everything in the homes was covered with a very fine dust, like it had been a long time since they were there. There was no apparent presence of weapons. There seemed to be no destruction or breakage, and no evidence of any violence. Everything about them seemed peaceful. It was a mystery!

The team searched a large area of the city and found no evidence of any life other than vegetative. So, the next day several teams were to be deployed, and Karlson was going with one of them.

*

Karlson could hardly wait for morning to come. After a good breakfast, three transports left the starship for three cities. Commander Karl's team was to go back to the city that had already been somewhat explored, as it was the largest.

Sub-Commander Palants was the pilot and he offered a jump seat in the cockpit to Karlson, which the boy eagerly accepted. As soon as they had cleared the airlock, Palants asked Karlson if he wanted to stand between him and the co-pilot to watch. He was out of his seat in a second.

As they entered the upper atmosphere, Palants pointed out the readout for the outer hull temperature. The number was rising. He explained that the friction of the air against the hull of the transport caused heat, and the higher their speed and the thicker the air, the greater the heat. The transport was designed to be able to take a great deal of abuse, but they cruised downward at a responsible speed.

He watched as Palants expertly maneuvered the big ship through the atmosphere to the planet below. Being in the cockpit had great advantages ... the view through the large windows was panoramic—you could see all around, except for back (but there was even a viewscreen for that!).

They passed through a thick bank of pure white clouds. It was like being surrounded by giant cotton balls. Then they popped out of the clouds to see the great blue/green ocean below. Closer and closer they flew, and a distant land mass came into view. The white cities ahead sparkled in the morning light. As they passed over the land, they could see long white roads crisscross across the open fields and through lush green forests to the many cities below.

Karlson carefully watched Palants as he skillfully slowed the transport and began descending toward the outskirts of the city. The transport landed in nearly the same spot as before. Their crew consisted of twelve: Pilot Palants, Co-Pilot, Team Leader Commander Karl, five scientists, 3 crewmen, and Karlson. In the cargo bay they also had two flyers aboard for extended exploration.

Everyone except for the pilots exited the ship. Karlson stood at the top of the steps and took a deep breath. The cool air smelled fresh and sweet! His dad's voice behind him said, "Got a surprise for you. Look over there at the cargo hatch." Karlson looked and saw a crewman rolling a bright blue bicycle down the cargo ramp.

"My bike!" Karlson exclaimed, hardly believing his eyes. "You brought my bike with us on the ship?"

"Sure did. I haven't mentioned it to you because there was no place for you to ride it until now."

"Wow! Thanks, Dad! I can't believe it!" The boy grinned excitedly as he ran down the ramp. Karlson thanked the crewman who rolled the bike to him, and then he hopped on it and rode around the transport.

"You can ride in the city over there, but don't go far," his dad called to him.

Karlson nodded and replied happily, "Yes, sir," and then he was off!

*

The breeze swept his hair back off his forehead as he pedaled faster and faster. Shuttles, transports, and starships are terrific, but my bike is all *mine*! Soon he was passing through the wide decorative arch into the city. "Whoooo hoooo!" he shouted.

He rode down the main wide street, past the big beautiful pure white buildings and past the many parked vehicles along the road. He felt like he could ride a hundred miles, but only went one mile before he turned back; he had promised his father that he wouldn't go too far. However, on the way back, he weaved in and out of side streets passing many vacant homes.

Curiosity got the best of him as he circled around and around in a cul-de-sac at the end of a street. One of the houses there looked different than the rest. It had, what appeared to be, toys on the small front lawn. Karlson carefully laid his bike down, and walked toward the brightly colored things in the dead grass. He picked them up. They were several rings about twelve inches wide. They looked like some kind of game pieces, like rings in "ring toss." He put them back down and stood quietly. This was someone's home. Probably with kids. But where are they? What happened to them?

He walked up the walkway toward the home. The front porch was decorated all around with filigree. Karlson stopped and touched it. The workmanship was beautiful. He put his fingers through the delicate airy carvings. No webs... or anything indicating insects. The front door stood open. The top of the doorway was very high ... these people were *way* taller than the Star People.

He dared to enter the silent house. Light streamed through the many windows. The room was large and full of comfortable looking furniture—really big furniture, compared to him. He walked to a wall that was covered with photographs ... kids ... plus parents with kids. There was even a baby ... with its short white hair tied up in the center of its little head. The smiling family looked very happy.

He then went into the other rooms. One was obviously a kitchen, and another was a weird bathroom (he guessed) and the other two were bedrooms. One was full of toys with three beds. He picked up a doll ... a white haired doll. Then he picked up a bright red toy "car." He looked around the room. If it weren't for the large size of everything, this could be a home from his own world.

He suddenly felt like an intruder. He put the toys down, turned, and left. He regretted the faint footprints he had made in the fine dust on the floor. This was a sad place ... beautiful, but sad.

He picked up his bike and began riding back to the transport. Getting a little tired, he stopped again and leaned his bike against a big round stone planter that was full of weeds instead of flowers. He hopped up and sat on the ledge around it. He looked about; everything was still so quiet. He took a few swallows of water from the container hooked to his belt. After a few minutes, he heard a slight hum that grew louder—it was one of the flyers passing overhead. Then the city was silent again except for the gentle breeze making a small scraping noise as it walked a dead leaf across the white pavement.

Then he heard something else ... or did he? A click. Did he really hear it? Silence. Click. There it was again! He *did* hear something! It was coming from the alley space between two buildings behind him. He quietly slipped off the planter ledge and started toward the alley. As far as he could see, there was nothing down it, and certainly nothing was moving. He carefully walked between the two pure white buildings. His footsteps made little sound. Still nothing.

The end of the alley opened upon a grassy area with white stone tables and seats; probably a nice flower garden at one time. But now, the tall mostly dead grass reached nearly to the tops of the chair seats, and the empty flower bins overflowed with dead weeds. There was a lovely tall white stone wall at the rear of the garden that, instead of being straight, was curved ... and not just plainly curved, it curved in and out, like a gently wave. The wall was very pretty, with its pure white stones held together with pale pink cement. Karlson was about to turn and leave, but he saw something small and dark dash through the dead grass and into the base of the white wall!

What was it! Where did it go? He cautiously crept up to the place where the small black thing had disappeared. The wall was solid stone, so where was it? He looked around into the grass ... had he just imagined it? Then he realized ... the wall *wasn't* solid at all! There was an opening! It was a narrow tall opening, cleverly hidden—an optical illusion that was made with the curvature of the wall and the stones. It made a slit that remained invisible unless you were standing right at it!

He peered into the passage within. He could see a ramp inside that descended down into the darkness. He unhooked the flashlight from his belt and turned it on into the slit. All he saw were smooth walls and more of the descending ramp. He didn't dare go inside. He had to call this in. There *was* something alive here after all—that black moving thing! And the hidden passage might give clues about the mysterious inhabitants of this seemingly deserted world.

*

Karlson called the transport on his radio to report his find, and in no time at all, the huge craft hovered overhead, and then smoothly descended between the tall fairy-land spires onto the wide street below. Everyone onboard the transport, except for the pilots, excitedly left the ship and came running up to the waiting Junior Cadet. Then the two flyers also landed and the people in them joined the group.

"Son, where is it?" Karl asked.

"Down here!" He led them down the alley and toward the white and pink gently curved wall.

"Where's the opening? I don't see a thing!" said one of the scientists.

Karlson ran ahead. "Here!" he pointed to the slit.

"Where?" the puzzled people said as they approached the hidden opening.

"Here!" the boy repeated.

"Well, I'll be a ..." one of the men started to say. "It really *is* invisible until you get right up on it!"

"I still don't see it ... whoa!" The last man said as he walked up. "There it is! This is remarkable!"

They shined their more powerful lights inside the strange opening, but again, all they saw was more ramp leading downward. Karl ordered two crewmen to return to the transport and bring back ten headsets equipped with radios, cameras, and lights, plus a couple of area illuminators. As soon as they returned, they all put on the headsets and performed an equipment check. On the transport, Sub-Commander Palants confirmed reception from each, except that Junior Cadet Karlson's video transmission was ... crooked. Karl adjusted the too-big set as best he could on the boy's head.

"Let's have two people stay out here and wait for us," Karl said. He looked at the narrow opening and then looked at the team ... and chose the two heaviest of the three crewmen to remain behind. The team of eight entered the slit—five scientists (three of which were ladies) one crewman, Karl, and Karlson. Into the darkness they went, one by one squeezing through the narrow slit, except for Karlson who fit easily.

Down they went in single file, their headset lights flashing off the dark walls. The air was still and dank. They must have descended about 20 feet before the ramp leveled into a large underground room. The crewman, carrying one of the area illuminators, set it down and turned it on, instantly lighting the entire space.

They all looked around in surprise. Lining the gray stone walls were, what appeared to be, beds ... more like bunk beds, as there were three per stack. Where there were no beds, there were strong shelves with containers on them, some small, some large. A bit away from the walls were simple tables and chairs. From the ceiling hung round orbs which were probably lights.

One of the scientists said, "This looks like a shelter of some kind."

The others agreed.

"Let's spread out," Karl said.

They each approached an area of the room, with their headset cameras sending the video back to the transport, which Palants

204

then transmitted to the ship. The team began talking among themselves:

"It looks like this place has been deserted for quite some time, just like the city."

"The city is so beautiful, why would they need to have a shelter?"

"Maybe they needed to hide from something."

"We have seen no evidence of any kind of struggle or destruction."

"So far ...."

"We need samples of this ... looks like food."

"Does anyone see a power source for the lights? I guess that's what those round things are that are hanging from the overhead."

"Nothing, so far."

"Over here!" called a scientist. They all gathered to where he was pointing to the floor. There was a bag that had evidently fallen and popped open, spewing some kind of dried beans about. But that wasn't what was interesting ... it was the marks of something that had disturbed the beans ... like some sort of small animal.

"Maybe that is from what I saw run in here," Karlson suggested. "It was small and black, and it might have been hairy."

"Everyone be on the lookout ... we may not be alone down here." No sooner than Karl had said the words, a small black ... coconut ... ran along the edge of the room and disappeared up the ramp!

Karl instantly called the transport, "Palants, did you get video of that thing?"

"Yes, sir, I ..."

Then surprised yelps came over the radio. "What was that? It came from down there! Where did it go?" Evidently the small running coconut-looking creature surprised the two crewmen waiting outside the entrance to the underground shelter.

"Now we know there is at least one living thing, other than plant life, in this place."

"Did anyone get a good look at it?"

"Seemed to have four legs ... and hair or fur."

Then someone called out. "Take a look at this! It's a drawing!"

Everyone ran to and crowded around the scrawled picture on the wall. They all peered at it closely. "It's a drawing ... like made by a child," one of the lady scientists said softly.

It was an amateurish drawing, but clearly depicted a very tall strange insect-like being, with two large eyes and slits for a nose. With a great sword, it was chasing three small terrified children. The children were those of *this* world. The attacker clearly was not, because everyone staring at the unhappy scene recognized him—he was one of the beings that put their dead on the planet they had recently found. He was a Bug-man.

*

With the discovery of the shelter and new information from the child's drawing, the other exploring teams began looking for additional hidden shelters, and found quite a few. All seemed like they had not been used for a long time. The exploring teams also found photographs of children with the little creature that they had seen. They were evidently pets, and actually kind of cute— like little round-eyed walking hairy coconuts. It became apparent that the pleasant inhabitants of this fairyland-like world were invaded by the Bug beings. The lack of destruction (and bodies) indicated that the Bug-men easily captured the people and removed them. But for *what* remained a mystery ... possibly slavery ... or, horribly, perhaps for food.

*

Back on the starship, Karlson asked the High Commander (who was dining with them that evening), "If the people from this planet were kidnapped, and if we found them, would we help them get back home?"

The High Commander was silent for a moment, and then answered, "Yes, of course, but only if they wanted us to ... which they probably would. No one has the right to enslave another, if that is what happened here. Our policy is that we don't interfere unless we absolutely have to, or we are asked to. The only worry I have is that the Bug-people might be too technologically advanced for us. We would have to be *very* careful ... we wouldn't want to end up like those poor folks here did."

Chapter 24

Please Don't Die!

After exploring the beautiful cities, the scientists turned their attention to the second continent on the planet. It had no cities, or any structures of any kind. The first team went to the surface of that land mass in air-suits ... safety first. No harmful pathogens were found, and the temperature was warmer than the land with the white cities. So, the High Commander allowed groups to have mini vacations because everyone needs some warm sunshine, especially a growing boy. A very nice area was chosen to set up a camp. It was in the middle of a huge field of six-inch high grass. As the warm breeze gently blew across the field, the tips of the grass seemed to shift in color, from a light to a dark green. It was fascinating to watch—it looked like waves on an ocean.

*

Shuttles arrived with crew to relax for the day and then they returned to the ship, but Karl and Karlson decided to stay overnight with some others. They called it "camping out," but to Karlson, it was no different than living on the streets, except that this "camping" included tents and good food.

It was almost surreal seeing officers and crew wearing only colorful shorts and tee shirts instead of uniforms! Karlson was happy that his shorts, which he had originally brought, mostly still fit. Between relaxing and eating, they played games involving balls. It was lots of fun and Karlson enjoyed it very much.

The first night they were there, as they sat around finishing their dinner, dusk turned into night. The stars above were so bright! To see the stars even better, someone turned off the outer lights on the shuttle that was parked behind them.

"Look!" someone exclaimed. "Over there!"

They all looked where he was pointing. Off in the grassy field were small pink dots—about 20 of them. They glowed steadily, unmoving.

"What are they?" someone asked.

"Insects? Some kind of glowing bugs in the grass?"

One of the officers brought out a bright light from the shuttle and turned it on, shining it over the field. The pink glowing dots disappeared. He turned off the light and they reappeared!

The next morning, after an investigation of the grass in the field, they found nothing. However that evening, as dusk turned into night, the pink dots returned, but now there were more—about a hundred more!

Again, a thorough investigation the next morning gave no clue as to what the strange pink dots could be. All that was out there was grass.

That evening, dusk was coming on fast. The field was covered with a darkening shadow from the mountains in the far distance. Even though it wasn't completely dark yet, the glowing pink dots were appearing. They had increased! The field was covered with them—thousands and thousands of them!

"I gotta see what those things are," one of the crewmen said. He took a flashlight and walked toward the field.

Alarmed at the huge increase of the strange dots, Karl ordered everyone to pack up.

Karlson was about to fold his lawn chair and stow it inside, when his sharp eyes noticed something under the shuttle up against one of its supporting struts. He curiously walked over to it. There was something alive there! The last angled rays of sunlight shown through brown fluffy hair—making it look almost golden. It was a ball of fur!

"Hey there, little fella," he called softly to the fuzzy creature. "I won't hurt you ... hey ..." he called gently as he squatted down to see it better.

Then the cute little fuzz ball turned to him. Its pink eyes bore into his. Its thin lips curled up to show long and very sharp teeth. Karlson was shocked. It was a rat! No, it was worse than a rat! He remembered something about: if you are confronted with an angry animal, you should move away slowly. No way! He scurried backwards as fast as he could. The thing lunged toward him but stopped short of leaving the shadow of the shuttle.

The curious crewman had reached the field and turned his bright flashlight onto it.

"They're rats! The pink things are rats!" Karlson hollered. But his warning came too late. The pink dots suddenly moved very fast. They were all charging!

The crewman out in the field tried to turn and run, but instead was quickly overcome—covered with the awful creatures. He thrashed about—screaming horribly! The closest person to the shuttle jumped in and tossed laser pistols out to waiting hands, including Karlson's. Then they all ran to the aid of the dying man, firing their weapons at the swarming beasts.

Karlson ran too. He flipped the safety off, and fired in front of the wave of pink eyes charging toward them. He hoped the laser blast would scare them back, but no, they didn't seem to care. It would be nearly impossible to pick off one rat at a time, but they had no choice. The men shot continually at the oncoming rats. But it wasn't enough. As soon as you fried one, two more would hop over the sizzling body and keep coming with their glaring and determined unblinking pink eyes.

The crewman's screams were now silent. It was obvious that they couldn't help the unmoving man on the ground—his flesh had been eaten to his bones.

The pink dots kept coming—wave after wave of them! Karl ordered retreat, and everyone ran back to the safety of the ship. The last man jumped through the hatch as it was closing—and it wasn't a moment too soon, as they could hear the small monsters leaping and crashing onto it.

Everyone onboard was stricken with silence from the horror they had just witnessed.

"What the heck was that!" one crew member yelled out almost hysterically.

The shuttle pilot turned on the engine and the craft rose above the field. Karlson looked out of the viewport. He could see the rats falling off the shuttle struts while others tried to jump up at them! The shuttle slowly circled above the field. The rats below were so thick that you couldn't see the grass ... but you could see the rat covered lump that used to be the crewman.

The last man, who had leapt into the shuttle, started scratching his leg. Karl moved over to him. "Were you bit?" he asked tensely. The man stopped scratching, as those around him closely peered at his leg. There were two teeth marks.

*

When they returned to the safety of the starship, the injured man was immediately taken to the medical infirmary. The next morning, a team was dispatched to retrieve the dead crewman. What they found was a skeleton—his bones had been picked clean.

Then the real horror started.

The bitten crewman got sick. Then others got sick. Even though the infirmary quarantined the sick, the illness spread. The doctor was alarmed at how fast it was spreading, but he couldn't quite figure *how* it was spreading. The ship's air scrubbers should have eliminated any air-born germs, but it still spread like the worst flu ever. A then logical assumption would be that it was spread by direct physical contact. But that was unlikely because of the instant quarantine of anyone showing symptoms ... and it sure wasn't like the sick patients were running around biting everyone!

Then the doctor and the infirmary staff got sick. Then everyone got sick. Everyone ... except for Karlson.

*

Karlson looked down at his father as he lay helpless in his bunk. His healthy tanned skin was now a pasty white. His soft wavy dark hair was plastered with sweat to his head. His strong muscles lay weak. His handsome face was swollen—like he had been severely beaten up.

"Dad, what can I do?" the boy asked anxiously.

Karl's puffy lips barely moved. "Water," he said thickly.

Karlson quickly grabbed two bottles of water from the little refrigerator mounted into the wall. Karl painfully raised himself up on one elbow to drink. He could barely hold the water bottle to his lips. He drank one entire bottle and then fell weakly back onto his pillow, breathing raggedly. Karl barely cracked his swollen eyes open and whispered, "Son, help the others." Then his eyes closed, and he fell back into a tormented sleep.

Karlson sat on the edge of the bunk. Help the others, his dad had said. What can I do? Then he realized he could do what he had just done for his father. He needed water. They *all* must need water! He dragged a little table next to the bunk. He opened the other bottle of water and put it there close to his dad's hand.

The ship had lots of bottled drinking water. It was true that the ship recycled water from everything—showers, toilets—everything, then filtered and purified it to be used again; it was even suitable for drinking. But human nature has its quirks. Many thought the very idea of drinking purified toilet water as "nasty," so starships stored massive amounts of bottled drinking water, just to make everyone comfortable.

Karlson went to the galley (kitchen). There he found cases and cases of bottled water, stacked in a storage room. He got a rolling serving cart and filled it with as many cases as would fit on it. They were heavy! He rolled the cart down the passageway, first to the infirmary where he figured the sickest would be. All 30 beds were full. The sick people were so weak that he had to help each one drink.. He then set an extra open bottle on tables next to them, near their hands. He assured each that he would be back as soon as he could.

He returned to the galley for another load. He started at the nearest set of living quarters—the officers. The ship was so quiet, as he alone was walking about. Everyone else was bedridden ... everyone.

He figured he would start at the Captain's quarters since it was the first door he came to. He politely knocked and heard a raspy, "Enter."

The Captain looked terrible, but he had been one of the last to get sick, so he was still able to speak. He saw two water bottles in Karlson's hands. "Yes," he mumbled hoarsely as he eagerly accepted the water. He gulped one down. "Thank you," he said weakly, "I couldn't get up."

Then he drank the other. Karlson quickly brought in two more.

"How many are sick? I haven't been able to get out of bed."

"Everyone, sir ... I think."

He looked at the boy, "Are you OK?"

"Yes, sir, so far."

He saw the boy's cart. "Are you taking water to everyone?"

"Yes, sir, I don't know what else to do."

"You are doing great. I was dying of thirst, and I'll bet everyone else is too." He pointed to a big chart clipped to the wall. "That is a list of all the quarters on the ship. Take it. You can use it to be sure to find everyone. There are 121 souls onboard, including you." He pointed to the desk drawer and motioned for him to open it. "Inside the red envelope is a master pass key-card. You can use it to access any locked compartment on the ship." He fell weakly back on his pillow. He took a deep breath and then whispered, "Don't let anyone die."

That was a tall order—and an unfair one—for a kid who didn't know the first thing about doctoring. But Karlson had already decided to do just exactly what the Captain said. He would do the best he could—he would try to let no one die.

"Sir, I need more water. I've gotten all that I found in the kitchen."

The Captain took a large shaky breath. "Go to the freight elevator in the back of the galley. Go up to deck C, storage. You'll find plenty there."

Afraid the Captain would pass out, Karlson said anxiously, "Sir! Sir, what about the ship? No one is ... is in control!"

The Captain's glassy eyes turned to the boy. "Don't worry. Baring anything unusual, the ship will be OK ... it's on auto ...." And with that, the Captain fell back on his pillow and passed out.

Karlson continued his water delivery until he ran out. Before he went to the galley, he quickly checked on his dad. He was so weak that he hadn't touched the open bottle next to his bunk, so Karlson woke him and fed him water as best he could without drowning him. Then he pushed his cart back to the galley. He found the big freight elevator just as the Captain had said. He rolled his cart in and up he rode. When the elevator doors opened, Karlson saw a huge space, just full of supplies. There were big numbers high on the walls behind large groupings of items.

In front of him was a directory. He read down ... Water – 24. He pushed his cart to section 24, and there were millions of cases of bottled water, or so it seemed. Because deck C was closer to the zero-gravity hub, the gravity was less, so he easily loaded up normally very heavy cases and returned to his delivery rounds. As he pushed his cart, he did the math in his head. The Captain had said that, minus himself, there were 120 people onboard. At 10 minutes time each, it would take 1200 minutes to deliver water to every person. Divide that by 60 minutes, it would take ... 20 hours! Twenty hours to see everyone only once per day! When would he sleep? He felt overwhelmed. Then he reasoned that 10 minutes was probably too much time. If he could visit each person in 5 minutes—or maybe even less—then he could make two visits per day, which was really necessary because most were too weak to even lift the bottle and drink by themselves. Sleep would just have to wait.

He soon realized that filling his little cart from storage wasted too much time, so he rolled a large kitchen rack with big wheels into the elevator. He left his small cart behind. He figured he could load a lot more onto the big one, and use it instead of the little cart. With the lesser gravity on deck C, he was able to load the heavy cases easily, even onto the higher shelf on the big rolling rack. However, when he got off the elevator into normal gravity, the heavily laden rack was very difficult to move, especially with one of the wheels refusing to cooperate and roll straight. So, he used the big full rack to restock his small cart.

The ship was so silent, with only the squeaking sound of the wheels on his cart. Some of the compartment doors were locked, so he used his pass key-card and left them open when he left. As Karlson distributed water to thirsty lips, he became more and more worried. No one was getting better. What if they all died? He would be all alone on a death ship! He didn't have time to ponder that horrible thought because the red and yellow alarm lights suddenly flashed along all the passageways.

*

He ran toward the control room thinking: Really? As if there weren't enough trouble, now this!? As he neared the control room, he could hear an alarm beeping loudly inside. He entered and quickly looked around. There! A bright red blinking light! The proximity alert! Panic struck the boy. He remembered that the proximity alert warned of anything in the path of the starship— something that they might hit! He ran to the main viewscreen and set it to higher magnification. There! Something up ahead! A ... rock? It was huge, measuring over a mile in diameter, according to the readout. How soon would the ship hit the rock? What should he do? He reasoned: If I do nothing, we die. If I do *something*, it might be the wrong thing and we *still* die—or possibly not. The option of possibly *not dying* was the only option.

Karlson went to the navigation station. He found the directional dial and moved it one notch. He watched the readout. Nothing happened. Then he realized—the auto-pilot was still engaged! He reached over and switched the "auto" to off. Then he moved the directional dial one notch. The readout changed! The loud annoying alarm went silent and the flashing lights turned off. He waited for what seemed like half an hour (but was actually only about ten minutes), watching the rock get bigger and bigger on the viewscreen until the ship passed it safely. He then returned the directional dial to its original position, and re-engaged the "auto." He had saved the ship! Feeling a renewed energy, he continued his water rounds. (He didn't know it at the time, but

216

the auto-pilot would have turned the ship at the last moment, thereby avoiding certain disaster.)

*

The hours passed. Karlson's young usually energetic legs were so very tired. He could barely keep his eyes open. As he rolled his cart from room to room, he kept track on the chart the Captain had given him. He had found all 120 people. They were all in their quarters, except for the ones in the infirmary. Sub-Commander Palants didn't even recognize him as Karlson helped him lift his head to drink the water. The lady that made his old uniform called him a strange name, like she thought he was someone else. Trace seemed delirious, as he weakly tried to fight the water bottle, until he realized that it was water. But most of them were so weak that they didn't do anything, except to try to swallow the water they were given.

*

He had served the entire crew twice. He had fallen asleep on the carpeted passageway deck once. Get water, serve water—get water, serve water—get water, serve water. He kept at it. Get water, serve water. He didn't know how many days had come and gone. He thought about using tap water instead of having to get the bottles, but then he reasoned that there was no one to monitor the water purification system, so then it might be or become contaminated. So, he continued with the bottled water. As he emptied the plastic cases holding the water bottles, he tossed them aside in the corridors. He was making a mess, but he just didn't care.

The smell was getting almost unbearable. People were so sick that they just "went" in their bunks. The air scrubbers removed the smell of pee and poop in most of the ship, but the individual quarters just reeked. The air stunk so bad that the smell almost burned his nose hairs!

It was cold on his forehead—a big sword! The Bug people had found him! The sword was tugging at his hair. He had to get away! He moved and the hum got louder and continued to suck up his hair. He opened his eyes. It wasn't a Bug's sword at all; it was the automatic vacuum cleaner. It was against his head, trying to suck him up like he was a piece of trash on the carpet. He struggled to sit up; his arms and legs were so heavy with fatigue. He found the switch on the vac unit and shut it off. He wanted to go back to sleep on the passageway deck, but instead he forced himself up.

Karlson kept at it. Each time he had finished a complete delivery tour, he went back to his dad's quarters. He couldn't remember how many times he had made his rounds—it was just a big blur. He was so tired. As he gave his dad water, his heavy eyelids were closing. He plopped down onto the edge of the bunk and forced himself awake. As he watched his father's labored breathing, his lip trembled and a tear rolled down his cheek. "Dad, I love you ... please," he whispered, "please don't die!"

Chapter 25

Cadet

Karlson fidgeted. He nervously shifted from one foot to another as he waited. He wiggled his fingers in the white gloves that the lady down in "Ship Services—Tailoring" had made especially for him. He peeked through a crack in the curtain. The whole ship was out there! And all were wearing their dress-white uniforms!

The nervous lump in his throat got bigger.

Three weeks had passed, but it seemed like it was only yesterday—the nightmare of fear that he would be all alone, hurtling through space in a death ship. When he woke up from exhaustion, curled up at the bottom of his dad's bunk, he remembered how happy he was to see his dad breathing normally! When he had called to him, his dad had answered right away. He was better! They all were!

For his next rounds, he included a carton of orange juice for each person. As it turned out, hydration was the key. Had they not gotten adequate water during the worst of the sickness, their bodies would have dehydrated to the point where they all would have died. That's what the doctor had said. As the crew gradually recovered, with less and less needing his help in drinking, he was able to move more quickly from one to another. He raided the galley and added some solid food to his rounds. His "patients" even started calling him "Doc!" When others were well enough to take over, he finally really slept ... for about 12 hours straight!

His mind snapped back to the present. The High Commander rose from his chair and walked a few steps to the podium. He addressed the assembly with a few words, and then called "Junior Cadet Karlson!"

The dreaded moment had arrived. Karlson chided himself—Get a grip! I am a Star Man's Son! Dad wouldn't be nervous! So, he stood as straight as he could and walked bravely onto the stage. Breaking customary protocol, the High Commander saluted him first! Karlson was surprised, but quickly returned the salute. Everyone started clapping, including the High Commander. Then the assembled crew all stood up, smiling and continued clapping!

Karlson felt his cheeks blush with embarrassment.

The High Commander motioned everyone to quiet down. He turned to Karlson. "Son, you saved the life of every single person on this ship. You took initiative. You behaved, not as a child, but as a man." Then he said with an official tone, "Junior Cadet Karlson, on behalf of the command and crew of the *Explorer* Class Starship *Seeker*, you are hereby awarded the 'Star of Extraordinary Service!'" From a small box on the podium, he lifted up a ribbon with a sparkling gold star hanging from it, and put it around Karlson's neck.

Karlson did not know what to do or say. Then the High Commander stepped back and saluted him again!

As he returned the salute, he heard someone in the assembly say, "Saaaalute!"

Then the entire assembled crew snapped to attention and saluted him as well! He thought his shaking knees would buckle, but he managed to turn and return their salute.

The crew began to clap again, but the High Commander motioned them to be still, and then he continued. "And, on behalf of the Academy, you will no longer be a Junior Cadet," he said as he attached a gleaming bright insignia pin onto Karlson's uniform. "You are hereby now promoted to the rank of Full Cadet!"

"Congratulations, Cadet Karlson!" The High Commander stepped back and again saluted him.

Karlson was nearly speechless. Junior Cadets didn't reach full Cadet until they were 14! He returned the salute and said as manly as he could, "Thank you, sir, but I only did my job."

And with that, the officers and crew exploded into wild applause and cheers!

It was totally embarrassing.

He looked around and found his dad in the officer's section of the crowd. He was clapping harder than anyone else as he smiled with pride at his son.

* * *

Birthday parties were rare on a starship; they were rare like— never. But there was going to be one this time. Karlson would be 13, and this would be a first. But Karlson was now familiar with "firsts." He was the first child from his planet to be adopted by a Star Man. He was the first kid on his planet that knew how to pilot a Star People's flyer. He was the first person from his world to be going to the Star People's home planet. He was the first kid from his world to join the Star People's Academy. He was the first Academy Cadet to serve full-time on a starship. He was the first Junior Cadet to be taught how to pilot a shuttle. He was the first Junior Cadet to be promoted to Cadet before he even turned 13, and he was the first Cadet, ever, to save the lives of an entire starship crew. So, yes, there was going to be a birthday party—a great birthday party. The Captain and the crew wouldn't have it any other way.

The day arrived. Karlson knew something was up, because everyone looked at him and smiled; smiled like they knew a secret that he didn't. That evening after dinner, the lights dimmed and a gigantic cake on a cart was wheeled out of the kitchen. It had 13 big candles on it, all lit. (He guessed that starships did not stock those little birthday cake candles!)

Everyone started clapping and calling "Happy Birthday!" Karlson put his head down on the table and covered it with his hands. This was embarrassing! He quickly looked up, grinning broadly. What could he say? All that came out was, "Thank you, thank you."

It was a great evening. Gifts were hard to come by on a starship, but the inventive crew came up with some. Karlson received a scale model of the *Seeker*, hand made. He got a new chair for the dinner table. It sat a little lower (he had grown!) and had "Cadet Karlson" written in gold letters on the backrest. The High Commander gave him a High Commander's cap, telling him that it was for when he got his own command in the future. An Airman gave him a small hand-held video game, but warned him to never play it while on duty. Trace gave him a mag-belt, that he had re-made to fit the boy's waist properly—plus he promised no birthday spanking.

The Captain gave him a picture of a shuttle parked in the hangar; one that had been given a name alongside its number. Next to the 8 on the side was newly painted "Karlson." (He blushed terribly over that one.) Sub-Commander Palants gave him a framed official certificate, signifying that he was a Certified Shuttle Pilot.

His dad gave him a hug, and then said to everyone, "It was the best day of my life when I caught a starving little boy stealing food from our kitchen. He has brought me more joy and pride than I could ever have imagined. I couldn't ask for a better son." He kissed the top of Karlson's head, and everyone clapped loudly.

Karlson fought back tears. It was a great day.

Chapter 26

The Nebula

The starship *Seeker* had been exploring the unknown quadrant of space for over a year. Counting the time it took to arrive there and the several months time it would take for the return trip, it was time to leave and go home. Everyone was very happy. They would arrive just before everyone's off-world two-year duty tour would be up.

In the Officer's lounge as usual, Karlson and Trace sat down at a large table where they could spread out the day's lesson information. As Karlson opened his workbook for math problems, Trace said, "I heard some of the scientists talking. The long-range sensors detected a nebula that we were not aware of."

"What's a 'nebula'?" Karlson interrupted.

"A nebula is sort of a giant cloud of gas and dust in space. Some are really huge, but this one is smaller ... it only covers an area of approximately five light-years in diameter. Do you remember about 'light-years'?"

"Sure, it is the distance that light travels through a vacuum in one year, which is almost 6 trillion miles, so five light-years would be 30 trillion miles ... and you call that 'small'?" Karlson questioned.

"Yeah, kid, in nebula terms, it is small. Anyway, they want to go explore it, but Captain says we need to start for home."

"What do you think they'll decide?"

Trace shrugged his shoulders, "Don't know. Everyone wants to go home, so I am guessing that the Captain will win out." Then he changed the subject. "How do you think I would look if I grew a mustache?" he asked as he tucked a pencil between his nose and upper lip.

"I think you would look goofy," Karlson laughed.

"Yeah, you're probably right," Trace also laughed, then said with mock seriousness, "Let's get back to work. You fool around too much."

"*I* fool around too much?" Karlson just rolled his eyes.

*

Later, at dinner, Sub-Commander Palants joined Karl and Karlson at their table.

"Commander Karl, have you heard who is to be the pilot for the mission to the nebula?" he asked.

Karlson's ears perked up ... did he say "mission to the nebula"?

"Not yet, but I'll bet it will be you," Karl answered.

"I hope so. I've been studying the manual for that new transport. I sure would like to take it and try it out. You know, it has a star-drive engine."

"Yes," Karl said as he used his napkin. "It's a prototype; we were lucky to have it delivered to us when we started this trip."

"Dad, what's a 'prototype'?" Karlson eagerly asked.

"A prototype is an original of something new. In this case, the one we have onboard here is the first transport with a star-drive engine, so it can go beyond light-speed—just like a starship."

"We were to test it if we needed a transport to travel that fast, which of course, normally we don't," Palants added.

Karl interrupted the conversation as he rose to leave. "Son, I have to do a couple of things, so you can stay here for a while if you like, and I'll see you back at our quarters later."

"OK, Dad," he answered. "See you later."

Karlson watched his dad leave and then turned back to Palants. "Has it never been tested before?"

"Oh, of course it has, but not on an actual mission. That's why we have it."

"Where is it? I have never even *heard* of it."

Palants chuckled, "It's not a secret, we just haven't had need of it before. It's stowed in one of the cargo bays at the back of the ship. It's a bit bigger than the usual transport."

Karlson thought to himself: Bigger than the giant egg transports? It must be *really* big! "Sir, can we go see it?" he dared to ask.

Sub-Commander Palants laughed, "I suppose so, but I have to get permission from the Captain."

"Can we ask him now?"

*

Sub-Commander Palants liked the boy. He liked his honest enthusiasm for learning. He liked his polite manner and respectfulness. And, he missed his own son who was back home, so it came natural for him to indulge the boy. He called the control room and obtained the Captain's permission to give Cadet Karlson a tour of the new prototype star-drive transport.

When they arrived (after a very long walk) at the back of the ship, they stood at the hatch door to Cargo Bay C-3. "Ready for a sight?" Palants smiled.

"Yes, sir! Let's go in!" Karlson said eagerly.

Palants pushed the button and the heavy door opened. Inside was the biggest ship Karlson had ever seen, other than the starship. It did not look at all like a big long egg as the other transports did. This one was cylindrical with a rounded front, but the back was flat. The strange ship almost filled the entire cargo bay.

"How did they get this in here? It almost touches the overhead!" Karlson exclaimed in awe.

"Very carefully, I imagine," Palants chuckled. "What a monster!"

They walked around the gleaming silvery metal ship towering above them. They stopped at the rear of the craft and stared at the huge single star-drive engine. At the center of the flat back-end was the great circle, with a deep dark interior. Around it were six smaller standard engine ports, and they too were dark.

"Wow!" they both said at the same time, and then laughed.

"Those smaller engine ports are for the regular drive," Palants explained. "The big center is the star-drive engine."

"Yes, sir, I remember what a star-drive engine looks like, from when we went behind the starship in the mini-shuttle."

After a few moments, Palants suggested they go inside it. On the other side of the massive ship was a set of stairs leading to the open hatch high above. As they climbed the steps, the sound of their feet on the metal treads echoed in the silence of the huge cargo bay.

The inside of the ship was very different from a standard transport as well. There were front-facing comfortable seats as usual, but not very many. Against the wall between the cockpit and the rest of the ship was a science station complete with computers and all kinds of special sensor equipment. Above that was a large viewscreen. Karlson and Palants walked slowly down the center aisle toward the rear. Behind the seats were tables and chairs securely mounted to the deck. On both sides against the walls were slots for pressure suits. Beyond that, on the port side, there was a small galley, with storage for food and kitchen equipment. On the starboard side there was a bathroom—that even had a shower! At the far back of the ship there were a series of small compartments, each with a bunk, some shelves, a door-less closet, and a small viewport. There were ten of the weird little bunkrooms. The ship was truly a prototype. Normal transports did not have bunkrooms and kitchens!

Just then Sub-Commander Palants' radio came on. It was the Captain. "Captain to Palants."

"Palants here, Captain, go ahead, sir."

"Palants, the nebula mission is a 'go' and you are to be the pilot. See me tomorrow morning first thing."

"Yes, sir, Captain, I'll be there. Palants out." He turned to the boy, grinning widely. "The mission is on!" he exclaimed. "We're going to the nebula!"

"May I go along?" Karlson blurted out boldly.

*

As it turned out, a compromise had been made. The starship would begin the trip home at its normal cruising speed, and the special transport (they nicknamed *Nebula Seeker*) would detour and travel a bit faster to the nebula, take scientific readings, and then again traveling faster, catch up to and meet the *Seeker* that would be on its way home. The scientists estimated that the entire mini-mission would take no more than one week.

Karlson begged his dad to let him go. It would only be one week, and they could talk every day by video. Palants had already gotten permission from the Captain and the High Commander for the boy to go along—as a learning experience. But now, it was up to Karl, and he reluctantly finally agreed.

A whole week! Karlson packed several cadet uniforms, and lots of underwear. There were no laundry facilities on the *Nebula Seeker*. He also took his checker board and the little hand-held video game. There wouldn't be much to do on the trip there and back. It turned out not to matter because Trace was going too, and he was bringing Karlson's lessons!

*

The ship was stocked with food, and all systems checked out "green lights." The last things put onboard were the pressure suits for each person and then the people themselves. There were six scientists, Pilot Palants, a Co-Pilot, Trace, and Karlson. Ten people. That was the maximum limit for an extended mission, because there were only ten sleeping spaces. Karl had hugged his son goodbye, and said he wished he was going with them.

Karlson hadn't really seriously thought about being away from his father for such a long time, and suddenly had some doubts. But it was too late now. Besides, he reasoned, I can't be such a baby that I can't be away from my dad for a week! He kept telling himself that.

*

The great cargo bay hangar hatch doors opened to space. Everyone was in their seats except for Karlson. He had been invited by Sub-Commander Palants to sit in the cockpit jump seat, which he eagerly accepted. The huge ship quietly lifted off the cargo bay deck and proceeded to carefully exit the starship. Karlson turned in his seat to see the great dark star-drive engines of the *Seeker* as they passed by them. Then Palants maneuvered the transport away from the starship to a safe distance.

Palants turned and said to the boy, "Want to see something awesome?"

Karlson nodded, "Yes, sir!"

He turned on the ship's intercom and announced, "Attention everyone, watch out of the starboard side viewports. The *Seeker* is going to go to star-drive in a few moments."

Then he turned on the radio, picking up the countdown from the control room pilot of the starship: "Eight, seven, six, five, four,

229

three, two, one, engage!" The *Seeker's* six great dark star-drive engines came to life! They glowed orange then became an almost blinding yellow-white. The massive ship began to move, and then it was gone! It was gone like it had never even been there!

Karlson gulped.

*

The trip to the nebula was a bit boring, but Trace was there to make it positively annoying. He was bored too, so he made extra efforts to do more school lessons. He was especially fond of making Karlson do math in his head, which is always kind of hard to do.

One of the scientists was the cook, and one lunch-time he made the mistake of cooking beans ... the kind that make you have gas. The transport's air scrubbers had to work especially hard to clean out the continually-being-produced stink. The smell was horrible, and you couldn't even hide from it. The transport was big, but it wasn't *that* big! The scientist/cook promised them: no more beans! Ever!

It seemed like the mission was cursed with stink. Next, a sewer valve malfunctioned. The smell was worse than the farts. It wouldn't let the toilet and shower waste-water be recycled, so they had to dump all that into space before the valve could be fixed. Outer space was vast, so it was extremely unlikely that anyone in the future would run into the great glob of poopy mess that would be there just floating around forever and ever.

They were almost there. The nebula appeared larger and larger as they approached it, but at the same time, less dense. Trace explained that looking at it in the distance, the dust and gas seemed to have significant mass and thus a shape. But, the closer they got to it, the less shape it seemed to have. It was like if you were standing in a snow storm. If you look in the distance, the air looks all white, but if you look close to yourself, all you see are some snow flakes floating from the sky.

Three days had passed, and the *Nebula Seeker* slowed and stopped. They had arrived ... what a letdown. No big deal, Karlson thought to himself. Space looked the same as it always had ... it was just plain old regular outer space. But the scientists were excited, as they took samples of what seemed to be nothing. They had been taking pictures of the nebula the whole time the ship had been traveling, so now they were getting samples of the tiny, invisible-to-the-eye, particles that formed the nebula. They explained that the nebula could, someday in the far, far future, possibly form a new planet or a new star. Karlson listened politely, but still found it pretty much boring.

The next day, something new caught the interest of the scientists. It was a small section of the nebula that had not been really noticeable before. It was a spot that seemed to grow in size as minutes passed. All the ships sensors were focused on the strange reddish and purplish colored "cloud." Karlson watched it from the huge cockpit viewport. It was actually very pretty.

The scientists were at their computers and sensor equipment, murmuring between themselves over their readings. The large viewscreen above them showed the colorful mysterious cloud magnified. The co-pilot left the cockpit to go use the bathroom, so Karlson sat in his big comfortable co-pilot seat until he returned.

He glanced up at the small viewscreen on the control panel that showed the ship's interior. Trace was slouched down in one of the seats with his feet up on the seat in front of him, playing a game on Karlson's hand-held video game player. All six of the scientists were still at their instrument stations, and the co-pilot was on his way back from the bathroom. One of the scientist said that the cloud seemed to have significant mass. The others began agreeing with him. Karlson was about to get up and return to the jump seat, when suddenly the distant red-purple cloud seemed to burst! It was now coming at them—and coming FAST!

Pilot Palants' jumped, startled. He quickly looked at his instruments and then reached up and punched a large red button on the control board above him. An automated voice called out, "Incoming! To your seats! Incoming! To your seats! Incoming!" It repeated the words over and over several times.

Karlson tightly gripped the side of his seat as the ship turned harshly, throwing everyone and everything sideways. "Hold on!" Palants called out. Then Karlson was slammed back against the seat. He tried to straighten himself in the large co-pilot seat as the acceleration pressure increased. He glanced at the view-screen that showed the ship's interior. The scientists had immediately scrambled for the first row seats. Trace had dropped his feet and was sitting straight. The co-pilot had reached an empty aisle seat and was struggling to get himself into it.

"Boy! Is everyone in a seat?" Palants shouted out to Karlson as he worked the ship controls.

"Yes, sir! They are now! Eight seats!"

"You are my co-pilot!" Palants said between clenched teeth as he cut the normal drive engines and engaged the star-drive—at full power! The ship jerked slightly and then Karlson was squished harder and harder into the seat.

"Read out to me the blue numbers on the screen just below the auto-pilot!"

Karlson knew where the auto-pilot controls were. Below it he could easily see the numbers of the G force indicator (acceleration gravity force readout), which normally always reads "0" for normal acceleration with no additional forces.

"1.8 ... 1.9 ... 2.1 ..." It felt like an elephant was sitting on his chest! "2.3 ... 2.6 ..." He was just about to say 3.1 when his seat began to stretch out! It was like he was standing up, but also lying

232

down in the seat, and still stuck against the seat by the increasing acceleration pressure. He glanced back to the viewscreen. The seats in the back had changed as well and everyone was in a standing/lying position in the seat-turned-vertical bed. He could see fear in their eyes!

"What..." he began, but Palants interrupted.

"Seats go vertical so body flat—stand G force better—before black out." Palants gasped out the words. "Call out ...."

Karlson continued to call out the ever increasing gravity force against their bodies, "3.7 ... 4 ... 4.5," he gasped. It was getting very hard to breathe and talk. He glanced to the screen that showed the view *behind* the ship. The red/purple cloud was all around them! It took up the entire viewscreen! "4.9 ... 5.5 ... 6.1 ..." Karlson couldn't talk anymore. The pressure was too great on his chest. He fought for every breath.

Palants continued to control the ship. It was of no use worrying about instantly slamming the star-drive from neutral to full speed—something that had never been done before. The instruments had showed that the oncoming danger was solid or was composed of so many solid objects that it appeared solid, and it was coming at them at a speed greater than the ability of the ship sensors to register. It was either sit there and get killed, or try to outrun it with dangerous speed.

It was of no use to wish that this smaller ship had full acceleration blockers as the big starship had, instead of partial blockers. They all were going to have to suffer the increasing G forces. There was simply no choice in the matter. Palants' strong arms were so heavy that he could hardly move them. He looked at the speed indicator. The ship had already passed the limits of the forward sensors' abilities. They were flying blind.

It was getting harder to think straight. Their speed had now passed all records. They were going faster than anyone else had ever gone. Palants looked at the rear viewscreen. He could now see that the "cloud" was clearly composed of giant boulders racing toward them. Even at their ship's ever increasing speed, the massive cloud was catching up. He knew he had to stay conscious and in control so he could continue to try to outrun the cloud while changing course to dodge and avoid the massive rocks hurtling forward from behind them. If just one of those things hit them ... it would be all over. Their ship would be pulverized to dust instantly.

Karlson couldn't move his head, but he could see Palants. The man's face skin was stretched and pushed back horribly by the ship's ever increasing acceleration. He watched as a compartment on Palants' armrest flipped open.

"Tell ... this." Palants barely gasped the words out.

Karlson watched as a sharp thing came out of the armrest and injected Palants in his arm. Then the cockpit turned into sparkling stars. Then it turned to blackness. The boy passed out.

*

Karlson heard voices. He heard his dad's voice! Was he dreaming? He opened his eyes. He was in a white room ... on a bed ... that was *not* soft.

"Son, can you hear me?" his dad's voice said.

Karlson turned his head toward the voice. "Dad?" He was surprised at how weak his voice sounded. "Wha... happen... ?"

"Son, I was so worried. How do you feel? Can you move?" his dad asked anxiously.

Karlson took a deep breath. It felt good to be able to breathe again. "I think so." He wiggled his toes. "I think so," he repeated. "Is this the ship?" he asked as he looked around.

"Yes, you're on the *Seeker*. Your ship met us. Palants is an excellent pilot, to find us so quickly and to match speeds."

"Palants!" Karlson instantly remembered. "Where is he?"

"They are bringing him in now, I believe ..."

"He said to tell them," Karlson interrupted, "I think to tell them that he got a shot, an injection, from the armrest on the transport."

Karl's eyes widened and he immediately jumped to his feet and left the room. After several minutes he came back. "I am glad you told me about the injection. Palants gave himself that so he could remain conscious and stay strong enough to be able to continue controlling the ship." He paused and said softly, "It's a very dangerous drug. It is to be used only in the most serious of emergencies. That's how he was able to withstand over ten G's and still manage to remain conscious to save the ship from the meteor storm, then find us, and safely land in the cargo bay. It's absolutely amazing. He is amazing."

"Is he OK?" Karlson asked.

Karl was silent for a moment. "Son, I'm going to be honest with you. The doctors don't know yet. His body suffered great trauma from the hull breach loss of pressure before, remember? Now his body has been severely stressed by the drug ... which can be fatal. He ..." Karl paused, seeing the anxious look in his son's eyes. "He is in critical condition," Karl continued softly, "and he could die ... and if he survives, he may suffer from some mental or physical handicap as a result."

Karlson did not want to hear that.

"It is good that you told us of the injection so quickly," Karl continued. "The doctors may not have discovered that until later, so you telling us right away greatly improves his chances."

Karlson quickly changed the subject, as he did not want his dad to see tears in his eyes. He really liked Sub-Commander Palants. "How is everyone else? How's Trace?"

"Everyone else is fine. Trace has already been examined and released. As soon as they check you out some more, and if all is well, then you will be released too."

As soon as he had said that, a Medical Technician came in. "Your turn! Into the Med-Analyzer you go, young man," he said as he flicked the bed wheel-brakes off with his toe. He pushed Karlson's bed forward and into a big round tunnel thing. "Hold still ... won't hurt a bit!"

Karlson was not afraid. The lights were bright in the thing, so he closed them. He held as still as he could. After a few seconds, his bed was moving again, out the other end, being pulled by the same Med-Tech. "All done. See? Didn't hurt!"

The Med-Tech parked Karlson's bed against the wall, next to the door and went to talk to Karl. Karlson could see another bed being brought in. It was Palants! He propped himself up on his elbows, watching. Palants was pale and not moving. Several more doctors came in as he was wheeled into the Medical Analyzer.

Karlson's bed was moving again. He was going out the door. He tried to look back at Palants, but the door closed softly behind him. Sub-Commander Palants had risked his life to save them. He still may end up losing it. Karlson remembered how everyone had said that he was a hero for bringing water to sick people. That was *nothing* compared to this. All he lost was some sleep. This brave man may lose his life. Sub-Commander Palants is a hero, a *real* hero.

* * *

Karlson fidgeted in his new dress-white uniform. The fabric was stiff and it made his neck itch. This was a special gathering, so the lady in Ship's Services had made it for him. He sat between his dad and Trace in the front row. If they hadn't been up front, he wouldn't have been able to see much, because the whole ship's crew was assembled there.

The Captain rose from his chair and walked slowly to the podium up on the stage. "We are gathered here for special recognition of the heroic actions of Sub-Commander Palants. He knew the serious and deadly risk of injecting himself with the Pilot Enhancement Drug." The Captain paused. "He chose to take that risk, to save his ship and crew. Had he not done this, we surely would be missing and mourning our friends and fellow crewmembers from that mission. Tonight, we choose to honor that decision." He made a small motion with his hand and the entire crew stood up.

"Sub-Commander Palants!" The Captain turned smiling and started clapping. The entire crew started clapping as a motorized wheelchair entered the stage. Then the Captain broke protocol and saluted Palants. Palants quickly returned his salute, sitting as straight as he could in the wheelchair.

Then a voice said loudly, "Saaalute!" and the entire crew snapped to attention and saluted him. Palants turned the wheelchair, and returned their salute. Then everyone started clapping again.

The Captain motioned for the assembly to be still, and he continued. "It is not often that we have a promotion ceremony when we are so close to home base, but we will make an exception." He turned to the surprised Sub-Commander Palants and said, "For your extraordinary heroism, you are hereby now promoted to the rank of 'Commander.' Congratulations, Commander Palants!" and then he held out his hand that the shocked Palants took and shook.

Everyone started clapping and then called, "Speech! Speech!"

As they calmed down, Palants began to speak, "I am greatly honored by all this, and greatly shocked at this promotion ... and I thank you, Captain, for this great honor. But, in all honesty, if I may quote a young officer who is here today, I only did my job."

All the crew clapped and cheered!

Karl, grinning, looked down at Karlson, and Trace playfully punched him in the arm. It didn't hurt. As he and everyone continued clapping, he was glad that Sub... no, *Commander* Palants was his friend.

Chapter 27

A New Home

Karlson stood looking out into space. He thought about everything that had happened to him. He had been a starving orphan who got caught stealing food. The kind Star People had fed, educated, and most importantly, loved him. He had no parents, but got the best dad anyone could ask for. He went from being a little street kid with no future, to an Academy Cadet with a wonderful future. He felt that he was indeed the luckiest kid in the universe.

His father joined him in the officer's lounge. Together, they stood before the huge viewscreen. Karl broke the silence. "My parents and my sisters are eager to meet you."

After a moment Karlson looked up at his dad and asked nervously, "Will they like me?"

Karl was taken aback for a split second, then he smiled broadly, "Of course they'll like you! Everyone will like you, why would they *not* like you?"

Unsure, Karlson shrugged, but then silently thought: My father is a Star Man. I'm a Star Man's son. I'm the first of my people to go to the Star People's home world. This is good. He stood a little straighter with renewed confidence.

They were both transfixed with the view ahead—Karl, with longing to see his family, and Karlson, with a sense of curiosity and adventure. Even though the ship was slowing, they were fast approaching the bright blue planet with swirling pure white clouds about it.

Karl put his hand on Karlson's shoulder and said quietly, "This is our home. We call it Earth."

Be sure to get the next books in the
Star Man's Son series!
Star Man's Son: Discovery
and
Star Man's Son: Rescue

A note from the author ... please leave a review.

If you have enjoyed Star Man's Son, it would mean the world to me if you would leave a review. What did you love about the characters? Has the story inspired you? Would you like more books in this series? The number of positive reviews a book receives can make a huge impact on the book's success on Amazon. Thank you to all my wonderful readers for your support!

Made in the USA
Middletown, DE
08 February 2023